BERYL:
A Pig's Tale

by JANE SIMMONS

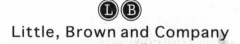

Ⓛ Ⓑ
Little, Brown and Company

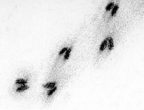

To Celia and Neil,
whose constant advice, endless patience,
and bountiful help made this book possible

Text and illustrations copyright © 2008 by Jane Simmons

Little, Brown and Company

Hachette Book Group
237 Park Avenue, New York, NY 10017
Visit our website at www.lb-kids.com

Little, Brown and Company is a division of Hachette Book Group, Inc.
The Little, Brown name and logo are trademarks of Hachette Book Group, Inc.

The publisher is not responsible for websites (or their content) that are not owned by the publisher.

First U.S. Paperback Edition: March 2011
First U.S. Hardcover Edition: March 2010
First published as *Beryl Goes Wild* in Great Britain by Orchard Books, a division of the
Watts Publishing Group Ltd., London, in August 2008

Library of Congress Cataloging-in-Publication Data
Simmons, Jane.
Beryl: a pig's tale / by Jane Simmons. — 1st U.S. ed.
p. cm.
Summary: Tired of being mistreated and cooped up, Beryl the piglet escapes her farm and meets a group of wild pigs, whose settlement splits up over the decision of whether to let her stay, and with her new "family" she sets out to find a new home.
ISBN 978-0-316-04410-3 (hc) / ISBN 978-0-316-04413-4 (pb)
[1. Pigs—Fiction. 2. Toleration—Fiction. 3. Family—Fiction. 4. Adventure and adventurers—Fiction.] I. Title.
PZ7.S59182Ber 2010
[Fic] —dc22

10 9 8 7 6 5 4 3 2 1

RRD-C

Printed in the United States of America

CHAPTERS

BERYL'S DAY HAD COME

Beryl sat in her sty. It was the only place she had ever known; she had lived in it all her life. It was the sty where her mother had lost her life when Beryl was born. It was the sty where she'd seen them take her father away. It was small and made of concrete and it sat in the corner of a huge, hangar-size barn. She could only just see over its thick walls to hundreds of other concrete sties. Beryl now shared it with her aunt Misery and her cousins.

The cousins didn't like Beryl and Beryl had given up trying to like them. It was something she had gotten used to. They sat in the opposite corner of the sty and stared at her, and she avoided their eyes and kept as quiet as a mouse, trying to appear as small as possible and hoping not to attract their attention. She spent most of her time daydreaming.

"The farmer's marking the largest young'uns!" hissed a neighbor over the sty wall.

"I wish they'd take you this time!" Aunt Misery grunted at Beryl. Her cousins sniggered, but Beryl was the smallest of them all because she was only allowed at the food trough after everyone else had finished. Aunt Misery glared angrily at Beryl. The largest of her cousins fell silent as he realized it must be his turn to be taken.

Beryl shifted uncomfortably and gazed at the familiar cracks and marks on the floor and the walls, hoping she would be overlooked. She peered out of

her favorite crack, where she could see things in the outside world, which always seemed so bright. She sat and watched the colors and shapes and wondered what they could be. She had often thought about the outside and how magical and mysterious it seemed.

She wondered what it would feel like to walk around out there.

The farmer strode down the alley toward her sty. As he came he slapped stickers onto the largest of the young pigs, and when their mothers wailed out in grief, he didn't seem to notice. He didn't stop or hesitate, he just kept striding and slapping on the stickers, *slap, slap, slap!*

"Hide behind me!" Aunt Misery whispered urgently to her brood and, at the same time, she thrust Beryl aggressively toward the alley gate with her snout.

Beryl swallowed nervously as the farmer steadily approached. However unpleasant her life with her aunt and cousins was, Beryl didn't want to be pushed into the limelight. With every stride the farmer took toward her, she had a growing feeling of dread. Whatever was happening, wherever the chosen pigs were being taken, Beryl sensed it could only be worse than where she was now. She had seen a lot of pigs taken, and they were never seen again.

Suddenly the farmer was above her, panting and swooping his arm over the sty wall, the sticker in his hand. Beryl gulped hard and squeezed her eyes tight shut.

SLAP!

She felt nothing! The farmer had stretched right over her and slapped the sticker onto the largest cousin's back.

Beryl couldn't help but feel a wave of relief.

"NO! Not my baby!" cried Aunt Misery, and for the first time that Beryl could remember, the cousins didn't say anything at all. They just went very, very pale.

Suddenly the barn doors creaked and groaned open, pouring light over the sties. Beryl blinked and squinted into the bleaching sunlight.

Two men with poles were shunting the chosen pigs out of their sties and into the alley. With all the pigs panicking and darting about, banging and crashing, squealing and wailing, the noise was deafening.

"I won't let them take you!" cried Aunt Misery. She pried the sticker off her son with her teeth, then leveled her cold stare at Beryl. Before Beryl could move, Aunt Misery lurched forward and pinned her to the wall. *Slap!* She stuck the sticker onto Beryl's back.

The men were bearing down on Beryl's sty, zapping pigs as they came closer. Beryl tried desperately to pull the sticker off. She twisted and turned, but as hard as she tried, she couldn't reach it. It wasn't her turn, she wasn't big enough yet! Aunt Misery and her cousins were laughing now, as Beryl frantically tried to rub the sticker off her back and onto the wall.

"Here they come!" goaded Aunt Misery.

The men reached Beryl's sty and swung the door open. Beryl froze.

"That one," said the hairy man, and poked Beryl with his pole. *Zeeezt!* An electric jolt ran down her back and legs. Suddenly there was nothing but pain and then, just as suddenly, it was gone.

"Come on!" shouted Harry. Beryl's head spun and she staggered, trying to find her feet. He stretched out with the pole to prod her again, but before it touched her, her mind cleared and she found her footing and sprang with all the energy she could muster into the alley and ran as fast as possible toward the light.

She was jostled up a ramp with the other stickered pigs. All around her they were squealing and panicking. Harry kept prodding with the pole and as he did so pigs screamed out. Beryl was swept along as she became part of a body of pigs.

Everyone was pushing and shoving, and when Beryl reached the top of the ramp Harry swung open some doors, pushing Beryl and the other pigs into the gloom of a truck. Beryl was squeezed in so tightly she could hardly breathe. The doors came together with a thunderous crash, and the last of the light was gone.

Beryl panted in the hot, stuffy darkness. All she could hear was the loud breathing of the other pigs. She thought of her father and how brave he had been when this had happened to him. As Beryl's eyes grew accustomed to the dark, she was overwhelmed by a sense of doom. She had no idea where they might be taking her—she had no experience of anywhere but her sty, so she couldn't imagine anywhere else. But she knew in her heart that wherever it was, it wasn't going to be good.

A ROAD TO NOWHERE

There was a spluttering noise and the engine roared
to life. The truck jolted and Beryl and the other pigs
stumbled this way and that as they bounced down
the farm track onto the road.

Beryl peered through a crack in the doors at
the magical outside world. It looked so gentle and
colorful and she wondered again what it would

feel like to be out there in the sun. Then the truck lurched and Beryl and the other pigs were thrown against its side.

For the first time in her life, Beryl wasn't in her sty; she wasn't with Aunt Misery and her cousins. But although she was relieved to be away from their bullying, now all she could feel was rising panic.

With a surge of courage, she shook off her shyness like an unwanted blanket. "Where are they taking us?" she cried to the others. "We've got to get out of here!"

The other pigs stared at her. Some of them began to sob and call for their mothers, but one large, gruff pig leveled his bully's gaze at Beryl.

"How do you think we can get out?" He frowned.

"I don't know," squeaked Beryl timidly, looking up and noticing the metal walls of the truck for the first time.

"Even if we could get out, where would we go?" the bully-pig said gruffly.

"Out there!" insisted Beryl, getting a bit of her courage back.

"In the wild?" he snorted, and some of the others snorted, too.

"Why not?" cried Beryl. "It can't be any worse than where they're taking us!"

"How do you know?" he grunted. "Have you ever been out there? Out there, there's nothing to eat. Out there, there's nowhere to sleep. Only wild pigs can live out there. We'd starve, or die of disease! We don't know how to survive out there. It has to be better for us in here, we're indoor pigs!"

"But what if they're going to kill us?" Beryl pleaded.

"They wouldn't do that! Why would they kill us?

It'll be just the same as before, maybe even better!" Gruff smiled reassuringly at the others. He turned to Beryl, the remnants of his smile disappearing rapidly from his face. "Out there, wild pigs would definitely kill us! They'd eat us!" he snarled, poking his face right up against hers. "You're mad, and you're upsetting everyone, so shut up!"

Beryl backed away. She sank into silence and timidity, but inside her mind raced. If she knew anything at all, she knew she had to get out of the truck somehow. Even if Gruff was right and they weren't going to die, she knew she didn't want to be stuck in another sty. Slowly Beryl was realizing that what she wanted was something new. Something exciting, something with hope, something magical—what she wanted was outside.

She sat with her back against the truck wall opposite Gruff and the other pigs. They stared at her, and she shifted uncomfortably under their scrutiny. Surely they must have thought about where they were going, so why were they all gazing at her as if she were dangerous? She sat as still as she could, looking down at the floor, and hoping they would forget she was there.

With a sudden screech, the truck lurched to the side. Beryl and the other pigs skidded together against one wall of the truck. A moment later the vehicle lurched the other way, and everyone slammed against the opposite wall. Suddenly Beryl was slipping backward. With a loud clang she was thrown against the truck doors. When she looked up, a wall of panicking pigs was sliding rapidly toward her. They smashed into her, knocking all the air out of her lungs, and at that very moment there was a loud *clunk!* The truck doors swung open and suddenly Beryl, terrified and gasping for breath, was flying through the air.

THE OUTSIDE

With a thump Beryl landed, tumbled down the road, and rolled to a stop. Dizzily she looked up and saw Gruff and a few others lying in the road. The truck screeched to a halt. Beryl pulled herself up onto her feet, staggering to find her balance.

"Now's our chance!" she shouted, but Gruff snorted and the other pigs just stared at her as if she were crazy. The driver's door opened.

"Hey! Come back here!" he shouted at the pigs, running toward them.

Beryl looked around in a panic. With all her strength, she made a giant leap toward some bushes, but beyond them the earth fell away in a steep bank. Head over tail went Beryl, down and down, crashing into the spiky undergrowth at the bottom of a gully.

"Hey!" shouted the truck driver again.

Beryl froze. Had he seen her escape? All she could hear was her heart thumping against her ribs. Not daring to breathe, she stayed as still as a stone. She heard a clank as he lowered the truck ramp.

"Come on, then!" he growled, and she heard Gruff and the others squeal and snort as they limped up the ramp to join the pigs still in the back of the truck.

The truck door slammed, then the driver's door, and at last the engine roared. Finally, the truck rumbled and creaked away into the distance, leaving the woods to fall into silence.

The thick forest closed around Beryl as she

realized she was completely alone. She licked the blood off a cut on her leg that was beginning to sting. A breeze swept through the trees, picking up leaves and swirling them around her. As the leaves danced, Beryl looked up at the sky peeking through the branches. What had she done? Whatever had possessed her?

Maybe she should have listened to Gruff. She probably *would* have been better off staying in the truck. She'd always been so timid, never saying anything to anyone, yet she had wanted to escape and now here she was, in the middle of nowhere all on her own.

Aunt Misery was right; she'd always told Beryl that she was stupid and that no good would come of her. Beryl felt wretched and scared.

Why had she run?

What if the pigs *were* going to a better place?

"Stop!" she said to the questions mounting in her head. She was here now, and that was all there was to it.

Gingerly, she stood up. She seemed to have aches and pains everywhere!

There was a rustle from nearby. Beryl froze. She could hear something moving around on the dry leaves. Slowly, she turned her head toward the sound. It was a tiny bird hopping around among the leaves and twigs, pecking at the ground. Beryl watched it going about its business. Then the bird noticed Beryl and took to the air, flying high up into the trees. Birdsong filled the forest. Now there were birds wherever Beryl looked, perched in the trees, in the air, and singing to one another.

Beryl started to pull herself carefully out of the gully, but the bushes had sharp spikes that gripped her skin and scratched her until she bled. She twisted and struggled until at last she was free from the brambles, but some of the thorns had broken off in her skin. She was scratched all over. Her legs ached and her cuts and scratches stung.

She stood panting with the effort of getting free from the spiky bushes. Beryl hadn't thought the outside would feel this way—wonderful one moment and painful the next. Through the crack in her sty it had looked so soft. She was frowning at the brambles when a strange creature popped up from a hole right in front of her. As she stared in surprise, it twitched its incredibly long ears in her direction. It seemed to be smelling the air. Fear gripped her. Beryl felt sure she should run as fast as she could, but she couldn't move. The creature hopped out of the hole, sniffed some more, and then took off into the undergrowth before Beryl had time to breathe.

Gruff's words filled her mind. *"We don't know how to survive out there!"*

"What am I going to do?" she sobbed.

MEETING THE WILD SIDE

A twig cracked nearby.

"Are you all right?" said a small voice.

Beryl looked around. She couldn't see anyone.

Out of the foliage stepped a scruffy little animal. Beryl blinked at it, trying to figure out what it was. The creature was very muddy, with a pointed snout at one end and a curly tail at the other. Under all the brown, strawlike hair and caked-on mud, it looked like a kind of pig.

Beryl's heart thumped hard against her ribcage as she realized what this strange creature must be.

A wild pig!

"Don't eat me!" Beryl cried.

"Why ever would I eat you?" asked the wild pig. "I saw you fall from the truck. My name's Amber."

"I'm lost!" squeaked Beryl as Amber came closer. Beryl towered above her. She hadn't imagined that wild pigs would be so little. Beryl stretched her whole body upward, to show Amber how much larger she really was.

"You can come home with me if you want. My uncle Bert will know what to do," said Amber.

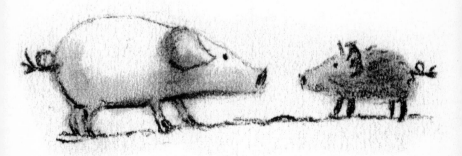

Beryl snorted. She didn't like that idea at all. If Gruff was right, she could catch something nasty from the wild pigs, or even end up as dinner.

What if that creature with the incredibly long ears came back and attacked her? Then her tummy rumbled—she was starving! She felt maybe she had no choice but to go home with Amber.

"OK," she said, and smiled nervously at her.

Beryl followed the wild pig, keeping her distance so it would be hard for Amber to try any funny business. As she stumbled along the track she kept stopping and looking around. She had seen a bit of the outside through the cracks in her sty, but actually being out in it was very strange.

"Who put all these trees here?" asked Beryl.

"I don't know. I think they've always been here," said Amber.

"It's very dirty," said Beryl. "Doesn't anybody ever sweep up?"

"Like who?" said Amber.

"The farmer?" said Beryl.

"Yeah, right!" snorted Amber.

Beryl didn't want to make this wild pig angry, so she changed the subject.

"How far is it to your uncle's home?" she wheezed. "I've never walked this far before and I'm getting very tired. The ground's got far too many lumps and bumps. Why isn't it flat?" She collapsed on the ground, huffing and puffing.

Amber frowned. "You can still see where we started from," she said. She began to wonder if she'd made a mistake helping this pork pig, but curiosity had gotten the better of her. She'd never seen or spoken to a pork pig before, though she'd heard stories about them from the other wild pigs. She'd always thought that they would be bigger, somehow. "You'll get used to it," she assured Beryl.

"Who put all these flowers here?" Beryl asked.

"Same person as the trees, I guess," Amber said with a giggle. She noticed how Beryl was looking around at everything, as if she had never seen trees or flowers before.

"Try sniffing one. It's a lily," Amber said gently.

"Sniff it?" said Beryl. "But why? What does it smell of?"

"Try it," Amber encouraged.

Beryl pulled herself up and edged around the flower. When she was safely facing Amber, with the flower between them, she gave it a quick sniff.

The smell was strong yet soft; it was summer; it was spring; it was the most wonderful smell Beryl had ever smelled. She shut her eyes and took a long, deep breath of it. At last she looked up at Amber with a delighted smile. Amber giggled.

"Do they all smell like that?" Beryl asked.

"They're all a bit different," said Amber.

The pink ones smelled sweet and the blue were really faint and delicate. Some of them hardly had any smell at all—Beryl had to bury her nose deep into them and give a really big sniff. Others she could smell long before she got to them.

Beryl forgot how tired and hungry she felt. She puttered happily along the path behind Amber, sniffing flowers to the left and to the right. She was so happy she began to sing as she sniffed.

"Sunny day,
Being so free,
I love flowers,
They're so silky."

"What's that?" asked Amber.

"Oh, nothing," said Beryl, going pink.

Amber stared. She had never ever seen a pig go pink before, and Beryl went seriously crimson.

"Tell me, please! I really liked it," said Amber.

"I made it up, but I'm not a very good singer," said Beryl, clearing her throat. "But I'll teach it to you, if you like."

After a few attempts, Amber joined in. Then she

made up a second verse. Together Beryl and Amber walked along the path singing and sniffing flowers, toward Amber's home and Uncle Bert. And Beryl completely forgot how tired and hungry and scared she was.

"Sunny day,
Being so free,
I love flowers,
They're so silky.
Tiddly tee,
Tiddly tum,
A walk in the woods
Is so much fun."

MUSHROOMS AND MUD

Beryl's tummy rumbled loudly. "I'm starving!" she whined. "How much farther is it?"

"To where?" asked Amber.

"To where we can get something to eat," moaned Beryl.

"We can eat here," said Amber, gesturing around.

"Really?" said Beryl, looking around. "Where?"

"Through here." Amber pointed with her snout and trotted off the path and into the undergrowth. Beryl hesitated. She watched Amber disappear into the bushes. Was this a wild pig trick? But Beryl's tummy rumbled again, and that made up her mind.

"Wait for me!" she called, putting her head down and pushing through the bushes to where Amber had disappeared. It was so thick that Amber and Beryl had to fight their way through. They heaved and pushed through the dense foliage and then suddenly burst out into a clearing, where hundreds of brilliantly colored flowers carpeted the ground.

Amber stopped and sniffed the air. "Yup," she said

with a sparkle in her eye. "I think this is a perfect spot for lunch!" And with that Amber started to burrow and dig in the soft ground.

Beryl stared at Amber digging and grunting in the dirt. "What *are* you doing?" she cried.

"Looking for lunch," said Amber. "Isn't this what you do?"

"Absolutely not!" snorted Beryl. She flung her snout in the air with a snort of disgust. "*I* eat out of a trough!"

"I don't know what a trough is," said Amber, and digging at the ground she unearthed a large, muddy root. "Look, it's really juicy. Try it, you'll like it," she encouraged, and pushed it toward Beryl.

Beryl's tummy moaned. She hadn't eaten anything since the night before, and for Beryl that was an awfully long time. At the farm the trough was replenished throughout the day, and although she had to wait until her cousins had finished, they never quite managed to eat all the food (even though they tried very hard), so Beryl had never really gone hungry. She edged suspiciously toward the root. What if this little pig was trying to poison her? She looked at Amber, who was lazily chewing at a bit of the root that had broken off.

Beryl felt relieved—if Amber was eating it, it must be all right. She took a deep breath, closed her eyes, and sank her teeth deep into the root.

The juice from the root filled Beryl's mouth. It was so sweet, it was as though Beryl had never tasted anything before in her life. And in a way, she hadn't;

the pellets at the farm were tasteless. The flavor of the root took Beryl over. She could have been anywhere, with anyone, it would have made no difference; she was drifting on a cloud, high up in the sky. The only thing in the whole world to Beryl was the sweet flavor of the juicy root. She chewed and chewed and chewed. At last she opened her eyes and looked at Amber with droopy eyelids and a lopsided smile.

"Do they all taste like that?" she asked.

"Sort of," said Amber, smiling. "Look, here's a mushroom. You have to be careful of these...'cause some of them are poisonous."

As they wandered along in the sun, munching, Beryl let its rays melt her aches away. She loved the warmth of the sun on her back as she strolled  along. But as it got stronger and hotter, her skin began to get pinker and pinker.

"It's awfully hot," she panted after a while.

"You're getting sunburned," said Amber. "I know just the thing."

She led Beryl down to a stream with a wide, muddy bank. Amber waded into the mud up to her belly.

"I don't think I want to go in there," said Beryl warily. Her skin was feeling very hot and prickly.

"Trust me, it's lovely." Amber smiled.

Although Amber seemed to be kind, Beryl still didn't really trust this little wild pig. She decided to keep her distance, going in a bit upstream, so Amber couldn't ambush her if she got stuck in the mud. Gingerly, she took her first steps into the mud. It was *very* cold. But as it reached her sunburned skin it took all the heat out of it. Soon she was deep in the mud and rolling about.

It was so cool and soothing, it took her painful sunburn right away.

"It's so wonderful!" she sighed. "Does it always feel like this?"

"No," said Amber, frowning. "Sometimes it's awful!"

"Really?" gasped Beryl.

"No!" said Amber, laughing.

They puttered back up to the path, Beryl stopping for a few more mushrooms. She tried to dig up a root, but her snout, unaccustomed to digging, was too sore, so Amber dug it up for her. Suddenly Beryl realized they were standing close enough to touch. Amber smiled at her and Beryl relaxed.

"Your nose'll get used to it," encouraged Amber gently. "We're nearly home now; it's just through that archway."

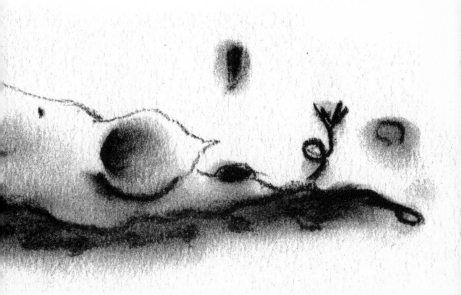

AMBER'S HOME

They stopped in the archway. Beryl had a good view over the whole settlement.

"You live here?" she said. She hadn't really thought about what Amber's home would be like. So very different from the farm, it was just an area hollowed out of the forest. There were no buildings or walls or gates or concrete.

"It looks lovely," Beryl said.

"Isn't it the same as yours?" asked Amber.

"NO!" said Beryl. She went on to tell Amber about the farm, Aunt Misery, and her cousins, the farmer and the truck, Gruff and the other pigs, and finally, her lucky escape.

As she came to the end of her story, Beryl looked up. Amber was staring at her in stunned silence. It was quite some time before Amber could say anything at all.

"That's awful," she said at last. "Where do you think they were taking you?"

"I don't know," said Beryl. It seemed so long ago now. She thought about Gruff and the others and wondered what might have happened to them.

"At least you're safe now. And you can come and live with us," Amber said, smiling.

"Us?" asked Beryl. "Oh, with your mom, you mean."

"No, she's dead," said Amber. Then looking at Beryl, she added quickly, "I didn't know her. She died when I was born."

"My mom died, too!" said Beryl excitedly, then realizing it sounded as if she was glad her mother was dead when really she meant she was glad that she and Amber had something in common. She added, "I didn't know my mom either. She died when I was born, too."

"Then we'll be sisters," said Amber, smiling.

"Yes!" Beryl beamed. "That's why we look so alike!" They both giggled.

Suddenly Beryl stopped as a thought hit her. "How many sisters and brothers have you got?" she asked warily. She didn't know any other pigs, apart from herself, who didn't have brothers or sisters.

"None! I'm an only pig," said Amber.

"Me, too!" said Beryl. "We really are alike!"

"Twins!" laughed Amber, and Beryl burst out laughing, too. They both laughed and chuckled together. Beryl had never laughed so much in her life, and tears welled up in her eyes. She laughed and laughed until her ribs hurt and she could hardly catch her breath. After a while she didn't even know why she was laughing, it just felt so good. All the stress and tension melted away as her shoulders shook and shook. Eventually it subsided and Beryl was left exhausted. She and Amber leaned on each other, gasping for breath and still letting the odd chuckle out.

They stayed like that until they were breathing evenly at last.

As they stood under the arch, recovering, something unsettling occurred to Beryl. "How many pigs did you say you lived with?" she asked Amber soberly.

"I didn't. I can count them up if you want," Amber replied merrily, and started to count in her head.

But just then, a large wild pig came wandering into view. Beryl tried to duck behind Amber.

"Oh my goodness! It's huge!" squealed Beryl, peeking out from behind Amber. "That's a real wild pig! Not like you, you're little and cute. That's a wild, wild pig! Look at its huge pointed tusks! It's enormous and ugly and savage! It's the sort of wild pig I was warned about! It'll tear me into little bits and eat me up! It'll give me the plague! I can't possibly stay here!" she cried with terror, looking into Amber's eyes.

Amber grunted unhappily.

"That's my uncle Bert!"

UNCLE BERT

"Come on, he won't eat you!" Amber said. Even though Beryl seriously doubted this, she realized she had little choice but to trust her new friend. She followed Amber hesitantly down into the settlement.

"Hello, Uncle Bert, this is Beryl. She's come to stay with us," said Amber.

"Hello, my dear," said Uncle Bert.

Beryl peeked out from behind Amber.

"Hello," she said nervously.

"Oh dear," said Uncle Bert as he saw Beryl properly. "This'll put the cat among the pigeons. I'm afraid you can't stay here, my dear. I know it must seem unfriendly, but you see, as pigs keep telling me, rules are rules."

"What do you mean?" asked Amber.

"You know the rules, Amber," said Uncle Bert. "Whatever I might think of them, apparently they are there to protect us. Rule Number One: 'No other type of animals allowed into the settlement.'"

"But Beryl's a pig, Uncle Bert!" cried Amber. "She's not another type of animal. Look at her! She's been through a terrible time. She's motherless—we're motherless sisters. She needs our help!"

"But the rules are the rules, Amber, however stupid they may be." Uncle Bert gave Beryl a kind smile. "What must you think of us, my dear?" His whole face lit up with a mischievous twinkle. Beryl found it impossible to be frightened of this kindly, stocky boar.

"It's not fair!" said Amber.

"You're quite right, of course, Amber. Come on, we'd better talk about it somewhere more private. We'll go to my den." He looked around nervously. "You have to realize it's not as simple as just bending the rules—it's much more difficult than that."

They trotted off behind him toward his den, Uncle

Bert looking anxiously around the whole time. But just before they reached the den entrance, another large wild pig came ambling into the settlement.

Beryl had been scared of Amber at first, and frightened of Uncle Bert from afar, but this new pig had a really dangerous air about it that Beryl couldn't ignore. The hairs on her back rose and she felt her whole body stiffen. He had a belligerent gait as he stomped into sight. There was something so grimly unpleasant about this pig that he seemed to give off waves of badness. They rolled over to Beryl like a rotten stench.

"Darn it! It's that old boar, Gerald," whispered Uncle Bert, nudging them inside. "Come on, quickly, before he sees you."

Beryl quickly ducked out of sight with Amber, but they were too slow.

"Bert!" Gerald yelled. "What's going on over there? That wasn't what I think it was, was it?"

He started lurching over toward the den.

"You two stay in here!" whispered Uncle Bert as he turned to meet Gerald.

"What's happening?" Beryl whispered. Amber peeked out of the den. Uncle Bert and Gerald were grunting and snorting at each other.

"I can't hear what they're saying," she said.

Uncle Bert and Gerald were arguing. They were arguing heatedly. At last Gerald turned his back on Uncle Bert. He shouted over his shoulder: "I'll be back! You can't change the rules to suit yourself. We'll see what the Council has to say!" With a sneer, he stomped off.

"Oh dear," sighed Uncle Bert as he entered the den. "What a day it's turning out to be."

"Is it going to be all right?" asked Amber.

"Oh yes. I'll make it all right, like I should

have done before. This time things have got to change!" As Uncle Bert spoke, he seemed to grow larger.

There was puffing and panting at the den entrance. Amber said it was Aunt Sissy.

"I came as soon as I heard. That old boar, Gerald, is telling everyone all about it. He's calling a Council!" she wheezed. "Hello, dear," she added. "You must be Beryl?"

Beryl had only known one aunt, her aunt Misery, so she had assumed all aunts would be much the same. She was absolutely fascinated by Amber's Aunt Sissy, who seemed to be the complete opposite of Aunt Misery.

Beryl couldn't help staring at Sissy's soft, kind features and her open, honest eyes, and she felt herself warming to Sissy's gushing concern. Beryl totally forgot Aunt Sissy was a wild pig. Although she was hairy, her gentleness shone so brightly that Beryl barely noticed the wildness. Aunt Sissy was by far the most beautiful pig that

Beryl had ever seen.

"What's all the fuss about?" cried Amber. "Why is there going to be a Council?"

"We don't have much time," said Aunt Sissy. "Bert, it'll have to come out now; she needs to know! You'd better explain it to her. It's going to be as bad as before." She looked anxiously at Uncle Bert.

"Before?" asked Amber.

"Come and sit down, Amber, and you, too, Beryl," Uncle Bert grunted. "And I shall do my best to explain."

RULE NUMBER ONE

Beryl sat on a tree root next to Amber. The root had been rubbed as smooth as a piglet's skin after years of pigs sitting on it. Uncle Bert sat down opposite them, and even though the mood was serious Beryl couldn't help feeling a blanket of peace wrap around her. She had never met any adult pigs who had spoken with such patience and understanding as

Uncle Bert and Aunt Sissy. They treated her and Amber as their equals and she wished, with all her heart, that this could somehow be her home.

"It's all down to Rule Number One," Uncle Bert explained as he leaned forward. "You see, in the old days, well before I was born—come to think of it, before your grandfather, or his grandfather, or even *his* grandfather, was born..."

"Get on with it, Bert," urged Aunt Sissy.

"The first rule," Bert went on, "is Rule Number One: 'No other type of animals allowed into the settlement.' Of course, this settlement wasn't here back then. There was another settlement, the old settlement, over the mountain. There, the number-one rule originally meant no other type of animal apart from pigs, any pigs. But then the farmers came and set up farms nearby with lots of pork p—" He darted a guilty eye at Beryl. "I'm sorry, m'dear, I mean pink pigs. Some of the pink pigs from the farms escaped and came to live in the settlement.

The farmers came looking for them and took them back, but of course, by then they'd seen proper..." Again, a guilty look at Beryl. "...I mean, wild pigs. And that's when they started hunting them. They came and killed whole families, piglets, too, no one was safe. Some wild pigs managed to escape and this settlement was set up. And from then on, in this settlement, Rule Number One meant no other type of animal apart from wild pigs."

"Will the farmers come looking for me?" squealed Beryl.

"Oh, no, I don't think so," said Uncle Bert. "You see, farms are so much bigger nowadays. I've seen them—hundreds and hundreds of pigs, all kept inside, poor blighters. If one of those escaped, who'd notice, let alone who'd care!"

"Bert, the piglet's feelings!" scolded Aunt Sissy.

"Oh, I'm sorry, my dear, I didn't mean... Anyway, that was my argument before."

"What do you mean, before?" asked Amber.

Just then there was a snort at the entrance. An enormous woolly pig leaped into the den, followed by several other slightly smaller pigs.

"Oh, no. That's all we need," muttered Uncle Bert.

THE CHOSEN ONE

"So, you've come!" the large woolly pig breathed at Beryl, her eyes bright and sparkling. "We knew this day was upon us. It was in the stones!" she said, as if that would explain everything. "We are the Sisterhood of the Mystic Boar, and we welcome you!"

Aunt Sissy stepped in between Beryl and the

large woolly pig.

"Moonshine, I'm sorry to be unwelcoming, but I'm afraid this is a very bad time for us right now. There's going to be a Council, so if you don't mind…" She tried to usher Moonshine and the Sisterhood out of the den.

"The Council, yes! That's why we've come," gushed Moonshine, holding her ground. "It's a terrible thing, it can't happen again, not now… Not with this one… not with the Chosen One!" She looked directly at Beryl.

Beryl couldn't speak—it was as if she were caught in a spell. Moonshine's huge amber eyes and her broad, fanatical smile welded Beryl to the spot. Only when Amber brushed up against her and stood at her

side did Beryl feel the spell break.

"What happened before?" asked Amber, sounding irritated.

Moonshine, the Sisterhood, Aunt Sissy, and Uncle Bert stared at Amber as if they had been caught in the headlights of an oncoming car.

Uncle Bert shuffled his feet, took a deep breath, and said, "Well, yes, it'll all come out now of course, and you must hear it from us...."

There was a lot of grunting and snorting outside, followed by a loud stomping.

Aunt Sissy sighed heavily. "Just come in, Colin! We've been expecting you."

A huge ginger pig filled the entrance.

"Good evenin', all," said Colin, standing erect. "Terribly sorry to trouble you, but as Council Organizer, I have a duty to request your presence at the Council as soon as possible."

"Thank you, Colin. We'll be along in a minute," said Aunt Sissy.

"I'm sorry, ma'am, but I have been instructed by

the Council to escort you and Mr. Bert there myself, posthaste." He snorted, then, looking at his trotters, muttered, "If it had been up to me of course..."

"That's all right, Colin, strange times an' all," said Bert. He turned to Amber. "I'm so sorry, my dear, if only we had more time to explain."

"Explain what?" asked Amber.

"We'll tell you later," said Aunt Sissy. "Try not to

worry. Your uncle and I will sort things out."

"Can't we come?" asked Amber.

"No, my dear, I'm afraid there's a rule about that, too." Uncle Bert sighed. "We'll be as quick as we can."

Amber and Beryl watched as Aunt Sissy, Uncle Bert, Moonshine, the Sisterhood, and Colin shuffled out.

Amber and Beryl were alone once again.

THE COUNCIL

"Let's sneak into the Council," Amber whispered.

"But we're not allowed in, and I'm so pink!" said Beryl.

"OK, so we won't go in," said Amber. "But we have to hear what they say. It's about us, after all!"

They went into the round outside. There were lots of pigs, young and old, lining up at the entrance to

the Council chamber. Everyone stared at Beryl as she went past. She felt so large and pink among all the brown. She hurried along behind Amber, trying not to look at anyone, wishing with all her heart they'd forget that she was there.

Suddenly Amber stopped right in front of her. Beryl tripped and sent Amber tumbling into another small pig. Beryl went even pinker.

"This is my sister, Beryl," said Amber to the other pig.

Beryl grinned. She loved being called a sister. It really made her feel like she belonged with Amber. Nobody had ever wanted to be with Beryl before, and now she had a best friend and a sister all wrapped up in this lovely little pig.

Amber went on, "Beryl, this is my friend, Dew."

"I...I...I was really hoping to m...meet you, th...th...they've been talking about you s...so much!" stuttered Dew excitedly.

Beryl was still grinning. "Nice to meet you, too," she said.

"We're going to sneak a peek at the Council," Amber whispered. "Want to come?"

"Y...yes!" said Dew, and followed them into the woods.

"This way," Amber said as she pushed through the undergrowth.

"But there's nothing here except prickly bushes," said Beryl.

"Ssh! We're almost there," Amber whispered.

They squeezed through a small opening in the brambles and found themselves in a clearing. In the middle was a large hole in the earth. Amber crept up to it on her belly and peeked over the side.

"Look!" she whispered.

Beryl slithered up to the hole and peered over the

edge—she had a bird's-eye view into the Council chamber. Down below were rows of pigs radiating out from a central circle. She could see Uncle Bert and Aunt Sissy.

"Look, that's horrible Gerald," Amber whispered. "This is all his fault!" They all glared at Gerald, who was with a lot of large, mean-looking pigs.

"Your mom's over there," said Amber to Dew, pointing toward the Sisterhood of the Mystic Boar.

"Moonshine's your mom?" Beryl asked in surprise. She didn't think they looked very much alike—Dew was so nervous, whereas Moonshine was anything but.

"O…oh y…yes," said Dew, squirming. She was always embarrassed by her mother.

Down in the chamber one of the pigs next to Gerald started to speak in an angry voice. "The rules are part of our tradition—you can't meddle with them. If you don't like the rules, go and live somewhere else!"

Gerald and some of the other pigs next to him grunted their approval.

The Sisterhood started to sway, chanting in unison. "Mmm…it's in the stones, mmm…it's in the stones, mmm…she's the Chosen One!"

Uncle Bert looked very tired. "Surely it isn't right. Times have changed!" he said, raising his voice above the Sisterhood's chant. "They're not going to come looking for her. You can't turn a piglet out, not when she's so young. It's just not right! And it wasn't right before!"

A lot of pigs around him, including Aunt Sissy, grunted loudly in agreement.

"We have already bent the rules for you!" sneered

Gerald. "We should never have let that mongrel stay! Look what she's done now. You can't educate PORK!"

There was a lot of angry grunting and snorting from both sides.

The Sisterhood persisted. "Mmm…it's in the stones, mmm…it's in the stones, mmm…she's the Chosen One! Mmm…"

"What's a mongrel?" whispered Amber.

Dew shifted uncomfortably, her eyes darting from Amber to Beryl.

"Do you know something?" asked Amber.

"I…I'm not a…allowed to tell," stuttered Dew, and she started to back away.

"Tell what?" asked Amber, but Dew had gotten up off her belly and turned and disappeared into the undergrowth. Amber and Beryl looked at each other, puzzled.

"Dew, wait!" hissed Amber, and getting up on her trotters, she took off after her.

Beryl struggled to get up onto her hocks. As she stood up to follow Amber, her foot slipped, kicking a mound of dirt and stones down into the hole. A moment later they were clattering loudly onto the floor in the central circle of the Council chamber.

There were gasps from below, then a deathly silence. Beryl's heart pounded in her chest.

From below someone shouted, "WHO'S UP THERE?"

Before Beryl could stop herself, she looked down into the hole.

The whole Council chamber stared back up

at her. Some grunted and snorted, and then the shouting started…

"It's that pork pig!"

"Porks shouldn't be here!"

"Against the rules!"

"Throw them out!"

The Sisterhood chanted louder than ever. "MMM…THE CHOSEN ONE! MMM…"

Then, above all the shouting, snorting, *mmm*-ing, and chanting, a very loud, deep grunt filled the air. It rumbled around the chamber until finally everyone fell silent.

It was Uncle Bert. "Enough! Is this what it has come to? Calling piglets names? You should all be ashamed of yourselves! Pigs are pigs—there is no 'us' and 'them'—and there's no real threat to us from farmers." He seemed to grow larger as he went on. "This isn't about the safety of the settlement! It's about prejudice! We need to work out a better way for the rules to protect us *all*. And I, for one, won't stay where the rules are not for the protection of *all* pigs!"

Once again, the Council was filled with the sound of grunting and snorting pigs. As if an unseen force was pushing through the crowded chamber, the pigs divided into two groups, facing each other, shouting and grunting. Only Uncle Bert and Aunt Sissy seemed to remember that Beryl was still looking through the hole.

Amber crept back and stood by Beryl's shoulder. Uncle Bert and Aunt Sissy were looking directly at them. They all stood quite still. The noise from the crowd faded into the background. Uncle Bert, Aunt Sissy, Amber, and Beryl were caught in a moment all of their own. Nothing was said, but nothing needed to be—it was as if they were standing as one. They *were* one, they were family, and they were in this together.

LEAVING HOME AGAIN

Beryl and Amber walked back to the den in silence. There were no pigs in the round central area; the whole settlement was deserted.

Beryl sighed and flopped down on the soft roots in the safety of the den. She felt very tired. She closed her eyes and took in the smell and the warmth of her new home and wished with all her heart she could somehow stay here.

"I…I've been w…waiting for you." A voice came out of the shadows and Dew appeared. "I…I'm so s…sorry, I…I should have t…told you before, b…but I didn't, and then I…I couldn't."

"Tell me what?" said Amber.

"Y…you still d…don't kn…kn…know?" Dew stuttered.

"No," said Amber.

"A…a…about your, a…a…about your m…m… mother!" stammered Dew.

"My MOTHER?" Amber screwed up her face with disbelief. She couldn't for the life of her see what her mother had to do with anything.

At the same moment, Uncle Bert and Aunt Sissy appeared in the den entrance.

The word "mother" hung heavily in the air. Time seemed to stop. Beryl could hear nothing but her own breathing. No one moved. No one spoke.

At last Uncle Bert broke the silence.

"It's time you knew the truth," he said softly.

"Bert, not now, not here, we haven't time! We have to leave now, they'll be coming!" urged Aunt Sissy, looking anxiously behind them.

"We shall leave when we're good and ready, Sissy," said Bert. "We need to talk to Amber." Turning to face Amber, he went on. "This is very, very hard. Please try to understand why we've done the things that we felt we needed to do."

Amber blinked and sat still. She was stunned but trying to concentrate, trying to make some sort of sense of what was being said to her.

"I made a promise to keep a secret," he continued. "I could only break that promise if the settlement changed. Otherwise I would tell you when you were old enough."

"They're coming, Bert," whispered Aunt Sissy.

"This secret was kept so that you could have a proper childhood at the settlement," he went on. "Your happiness was the most important thing."

Beryl could hear grunting and snorting from

behind Aunt Sissy at the den entrance.

"Now the settlement is splitting, and we're leaving, but before we all set off, you need to know the truth…."

Suddenly a herd of huge ugly pigs pushed through the entrance, shoving Aunt Sissy out of the way. Beryl recognized Gerald's grim and twisted face.

The largest pig shouldered his way to the front. He reminded Beryl of Gruff.

"You, the mongrel, and that pork pig aren't welcome around here! We don't want your kind!" he shouted.

The bristles on Aunt Sissy's back stood up — she looked twice her size. Snorting loudly at him, she lurched forward.

"I helped your mother give birth to you! You
pig-squeak!" She looked around the group. "Tom,
I watched over you for a week when you had
the sniffles. And Eric, you were 'Eric the Boil' to
everyone, till Bert burst it for you. And you, Gerald,
we spent the best part of a week digging out your
burrow when it was flooded. There isn't anyone here
who can say we haven't done our bit for them!"

The group of pigs started shuffling and looking at

their trotters, somewhat embarrassed.

"I wouldn't want to stay here anyway, now!" spat Aunt Sissy. "Go on, get lost, we'll go in our own time!" The group of pigs, looking a lot less bullish, retreated outside.

Beryl peered out of the entrance.

"There's a lot more pigs out there," she said. "I'm so sorry, this is all my fault."

"Oh no, my dear, it's theirs, Gerald and his clan. And some of those outside, they'll be coming with us," said Uncle Bert. "You see, we're not alone."

"It's Moonshine and the Sisterhood!" Amber whispered to Dew.

"W…we must be c…coming with you!" said Dew excitedly, and she trotted out to join them.

Aunt Sissy suddenly looked haggard. A tear rolled down her cheek. "All our memories are here, Bert. I remember the day you dug this home out of the dirt. It took you so long, your back was bad for weeks. Our whole lives are here," she said, trying not to sob.

"Sissy, all our memories are in our hearts," said Uncle Bert. "This is just mud and roots, that's all. Wherever we end up, it will be better for all of us."

"I know that, dear," sniffed Aunt Sissy. "It's just I'll miss the place."

They took a long last look. Beryl had been here for such a short time and yet it was the only place that had ever made her feel safe. She had felt that here she could truly belong.

"It's always been too damp. Next burrow'll be a winner!" said Uncle Bert, winking at Aunt Sissy as together they joined the pigs outside.

Heads held high, they walked out of the settlement, followed by the Sisterhood and a few other supporters. At the main entrance they stopped and looked back. The other pigs gathered together and watched them leave. A few angry-looking pigs stood in a group with Gerald, jeering.

"It's so unfair. Why don't they leave instead of us?" asked Amber.

"Because they think they're right, and it's the Rule," said Uncle Bert. "We will start fresh, as we should have done before, and perhaps with a lot fewer rules."

Beryl and Amber walked along the path with Uncle Bert.

"I wish we could have had time to sit down and talk about your mother," Uncle Bert said to Amber.

"She's alive, isn't she?" Amber said.

"Yes," said Uncle Bert, a little taken aback by Amber's quickness to figure things out. "They forced her to leave the settlement. We fought with the

Council, but at first they weren't even going to let *you* stay. She wanted you to be safe, and she wanted you to live your life with other wild pigs. We all thought it was for the best for you to stay here with us."

"Why couldn't *she* stay?" Amber asked.

"Because your father was a pink," said Uncle Bert.

THE JOURNEY TO
THE EDGE

They left the settlement behind and began climbing up a mountain. Beryl was the slowest pig—even the very oldest pig and a mother with tiny piglets were faster—but no one hurried her. When they reached the summit, they formed a large circle to decide in which direction it would be best to travel.

"The Chosen One should decide!" said Moonshine

loudly, so everyone could hear. She was sitting with the Sisterhood, which started to chant "Chosen One" over and over. Dew peeked out from behind them and attempted a weak smile. Everyone stared at Beryl and she went very, very pink.

"Leave her alone!" shouted Amber, and the Sisterhood instantly fell silent.

Colin stood up. "I think we should elect a leader," he said, and sat back down.

"I think we've all probably had enough of leaders!" Aunt Sissy sighed heavily.

Uncle Bert grunted. "Has anyone any ideas about where we should go?"

There was a lot of grunting and snorting and the pigs started discussing possibilities among themselves.

Beryl sat with Amber looking across the valley.

"I wonder if I'll meet her now," Amber said.

"Your mother?" asked Beryl.

"I'm sorry, I guess I'm trying to get used to the idea of having a mother," said Amber.

"It's all right." Beryl smiled. "I'm truly really happy

for you."

"Even if I find my mother, you're my sister, so we'll share her," Amber decided.

"But she might not like me." Beryl frowned.

"Then we'll stay with Aunt Sissy and Uncle Bert!" Amber grunted. Then she softened and smiled. "But she is my mother, so she'll be like me, and I love you."

Eventually, Uncle Bert grunted again. "Anyone got any ideas?" All the pigs stared back in silence.

"The stones!" said Moonshine. "We'll ask the stones!" And so it was decided to let the Sisterhood do the "stones" ritual.

The Sisterhood formed a tight circle, noses in and tails out. They set up a grunting chant and began to sway to the haunting rhythm. "Grummph! Mmmm! Grummph! Mmmm!"

As the beat quickened the Sisterhood shuffled their trotters, finding any stones on the ground and kicking them into the center of the swaying mass. Soon there was a scattering of stones in the center, and the Sisterhood quickened the pace and stamped their trotters in time with the rhythm while the chanting and swaying increased. Dust billowed upward in a swirling cloud and the Sisterhood swayed and stamped and swooped and chanted around the ever-growing circle of stones. The pace picked up even more as the stamping got faster and faster and the chorus louder and louder, reaching a climax of frantic chanting as clouds of dirt and dust swirled high above the pulsating circle of pigs. And as it peaked, Moonshine let out a bloodcurdling cry that echoed across the valleys and up into the sky, and in the same moment the Sisterhood stopped dead.

No one moved a muscle. The swirling dust settled on and around the now still and silent circle. When the last particle of dust had floated to the ground, Moonshine lowered her head to the stones and studied them intently.

"Mmm," she said, as if choosing which root to have for lunch, "I think they mean…" She tilted her head to one side. "…That way." She pointed with her snout in the opposite direction to where they had come from.

"Hmmph!" snorted Aunt Sissy, but she started down the mountain and toward the forest with the rest of the pigs all the same.

At the end of the day, they made camp by the side of a stream. Beryl hobbled into the fast-running water.

"Do your trotters still hurt a lot?" asked Amber.

"A little bit, but I think they're getting used to it," said Beryl, paddling around in the cool water.

Beryl loved water. At the farm Aunt Misery had often told her off for blowing bubbles in the water trough. Here in the stream she was miles and miles away from Aunt Misery, and she could do whatever she liked. She sucked in huge mouthfuls and spat them out. Amber did the same, and soon they were squirting water at each other and squealing in delight. Dew came and joined in, and they played until finally they flopped, exhausted, onto the bank.

Uncle Bert came over. "Tomorrow we should reach the Edge. That's the boundary of the settlement," he said.

"I thought we'd already left the settlement," said Beryl, confused.

"Ah, no, that's just the center of the settlement—the village part, if you like. The actual settlement covers an enormous area. We need it for food, you see. It's shrunk a bit now, but it's still big. That's why Rule Number One is so ridiculous. We couldn't keep out every other type of animal, even if we wanted to—they need to eat, too! The Edge is the boundary to the whole settlement, where the great river runs. When we cross that, we'll be in the Vastness. Then we will start looking for a new settlement. Somewhere with enough land for food, somewhere where we can defend ourselves, somewhere where the ground is soft enough to dig out our burrows, somewhere away from any farmers." His brow furrowed as he concentrated on keeping the hopelessness out of his voice.

"The Vastness! But that's where the wolves and bears are!" Amber gasped.

"Yes," said Uncle Bert, frowning. "But we don't have a choice."

"Are wolves and bears bad, then?" asked Beryl.

Amber, Dew, and Uncle Bert stared at her, utterly stunned. A pig who didn't know how bad wolves and bears were!

"They are best avoided," sighed Uncle Bert at last.

THE EDGE

After a cool night under the stars, dawn broke and the herd of pigs crossed the stream and headed up and out of the valley.

Beryl's trotters still hurt from the day before. She became very tired climbing up and down hills—she wasn't used to all this walking. It was hot and they traveled all day, stopping only for food and drink.

Late in the afternoon they climbed over a very high, steep mountain. On the way down Beryl saw an enormous river snaking its way through the valley below. This had to be what Uncle Bert meant by the Great River, the settlement's boundary. This had to be the Edge.

When they eventually reached the bank, Beryl stood at the river's edge, letting its cool sparkling water soothe her trotters. The huge river rushed past, sucking at her feet, and Beryl marveled at its power. Sweeping over boulders until they were smooth and polished, the river swirled in eddies and whirlpools, pulling along everything in its path. Its sheer weight and unstoppable motion cut a deep channel through the forest.

"We can either camp on the other side and get it over and done with, or camp here and worry about it all night!" shouted a large, sandy-colored pig over the noise of the flowing water.

"The young ones are tired, Sandy. It might be better to wait till morning," cautioned Uncle Bert.

"I'd like to cross now!" shouted the oldest pig, and all the other old pigs agreed. The sows and their piglets were in favor of crossing then, too. Everyone wanted to leave the settlement behind them before nightfall. They turned to look at the slowest and most exhausted pig...the pig who could have dropped to the ground and wept...the Chosen One—Beryl.

Beryl couldn't think of anything worse than struggling across that powerful beast of a river. She was close to complete collapse. She was only still standing because it would take more effort to bend her stiff knees and sit. But they were only there because of her.... She looked into their expectant faces and took a deep breath.

"I'd love to cross," she said, smiling weakly.

The first pigs to go were the largest, testing the depth as they went. The current was flowing rapidly, but it was shallow enough for them to wade across. All the other pigs started to follow, the smallest and weakest herded inside a circle of bigger pigs, so they wouldn't get swept away. It was slow and difficult. Only Beryl considered it easier than being on land—in the water she found she wasn't the least bit heavy.

They had reached the middle when suddenly one of the outer pigs lost her footing and fell with a splash onto a piglet. The large sow struggled to get up, but slipped again, taking the piglet with her into a deep whirling pool. The water caught them and swirled them around and around. In a moment they were gone, pulled down the river by the current. The sow got wedged against a fallen tree trunk and managed to clamber onto it. She tried to reach the piglet, but it swept past her, squealing in terror.

Everyone froze. The piglet's squeals faded into the distance.

Suddenly, Beryl pushed off into the deeper water. She swam as fast as she could toward the piglet. The river pulled her along, weaving its way through fallen branches and rocks. The piglet had been pulled under by the swirling current. Beryl sucked in a lungful of air and dived down. Far below, swirling down and down, was the piglet. Beryl dived deeper and deeper, holding her breath. Air was being forced out of her lungs bit by bit. She was so close, she tried to hold on as she went down, but the last bit of air bubbled away from her, leaving her lungs hurting for more.

But she forced herself onward and, grabbing the limp piglet in her mouth, Beryl kicked off the river bed with one almighty swirl and shot up, breaking the surface with a large splash. As she pushed back up against the current, the little piglet spluttered and coughed. It was alive!

On the riverbank, the wild pigs were cheering with joy. Moonshine and the Sisterhood were rejoicing—the Chosen One would save them all!

"Oh, thank you, thank you!" cried the tearful mother, licking her piglet to warm it up.

"I've never seen anybody swim like that!" said Amber. "How did you learn?"

"I didn't know I could," whispered Beryl.

The tearful mother stopped fussing over her piglet and looked intently at Beryl. "I feel so awful!" she said. "I didn't want to come. I only came because the rest of the Sisterhood was and I didn't want to be left behind. I thought you weren't a proper pig and should have been thrown out. I thought all us proper pigs should have stayed. Now you've saved my baby, without a thought for your own life. I'm so sorry. I feel so ashamed of myself. You're much more of a pig than me—you're the most proper pig I've ever met, Beryl! Thank you."

The rest of the pigs had slowly made their way across the river. Now they were cheering, shouting congratulations and smiling at Beryl.

Beryl flopped down on the bank next to Amber and Dew. "What a day!" she said.

They were all exhausted. Aunt Sissy joined them. "The fun really starts tomorrow," she said, and winked.

INTO THE VASTNESS

The morning light spread across the valley and the mist danced lazily on the river.

Uncle Bert cleared his throat.

"Now, we have to find a new settlement," he said. "So it has been decided that three groups should go off in three different directions, and in a few days we will meet back here. The youngest, oldest, and a core group will stay here. My group will head up that mountain there, so we can see how the land lies." He turned to Beryl and Amber. "I thought you two might like to come with our group," he said, smiling.

"Oh yes, please!" gasped Amber.

"What about you, Beryl?" asked Uncle Bert. "Think you can walk some more?"

Beryl didn't know if she could. Her trotters still throbbed and her legs ached, but she looked at Amber's excited face.

"I'd love to go," she said, trying to convince herself, and Amber smiled.

Soon they were behind Aunt Sissy and Uncle Bert, trotting out of the valley with Dew, Moonshine, and a few of the Sisterhood.

It took all morning to get to the top of the mountain. When they finally reached the summit, Beryl gasped.

"The forest's endless," she said.

"I wish that were true, but we should still be

able to find a part of it for us," said Uncle Bert,
smiling. "I think we should go that way," he said,
gesturing down the mountain.

On the way down, once or twice Beryl felt
someone, or something, was watching her. She
caught up with Amber and Dew and walked beside
them. Cutting across their path at one point was a
shallow stream with stepping stones.

Beryl tried balancing on the stones, but she kept slipping off into the water. Amber and Dew found it easy and leaped from one stepping stone to another.

"I wish I could do that," said Beryl.

"Try again," said Amber, but Beryl knew she'd just fall off. Amber began to sing:

> "*Stepping stones, stepping stones,*
> *Jumping on the stepping stones,*
> *One, two, three, and four,*
> *Fall off one, there's always more.*"

As she sang, she jumped from stone to stone around Beryl. Dew joined in with Amber, so Beryl smiled and started singing too....

> "*Stepping stones, stepping stones,*
> *Jumping on the stepping stones,*
> *One, two, three, and four,*
> *Fall off one, there's always more.*"

Soon they were all leaping from one stone to another across the stream.

As they reached the bank, Beryl stopped and stared back, deep into the undergrowth.

"W…what is it?" asked Dew.

"I thought I saw something move," said Beryl. They stared into the shrubbery, but there was nothing to be seen.

"It can be a bit creepy in the forest," said Amber.

All day, Beryl kept feeling that there was something watching them. "I think we're being followed," she whispered to Amber and Dew.

"I…I feel like that, too, s…sometimes, but it's o…only the f…forest," said Dew.

"It's the wind in the trees and the branches creaking. The forest itself is alive," reassured Amber.

"I'm not sure. It feels as if something's watching us," Beryl said. If only she could be certain. The forest was creepy. The trees were the biggest Beryl had seen so far—they towered high up into the sky, blocking out the sunlight. Creepers crawled up the enormous trunks, snaking from one tree to another like huge twisted ropes. Even the undergrowth took on an eeriness—shrubs and bushes covered with lichen and moss closed in on the narrow path, adding to the claustrophobic density. Birds fluttered and rodents rustled in the undergrowth.

Amber was right—the whole forest was alive.

But Beryl couldn't shake the feeling of being scrutinized. Every step, every turn, every bush they passed, she felt someone's eyes on them.

"Are you all right?" asked Amber, concerned.

"It's just I still feel it," said Beryl. "Someone watching us. I can't think of anything else."

"Uncle Bert'll know what to do," Amber reassured Beryl. "Come on."

They caught up with Uncle Bert, Aunt Sissy, and Moonshine.

"Beryl feels something's following us," whispered Amber.

"I told you! I felt it, too! Someone's THERE!" cried Moonshine.

"SSSH!" hissed Aunt Sissy.

"We had the same feeling," said Uncle Bert softly. "Look, we'll make camp over there." He nodded at a fallen tree. "We'll keep an eye out and maybe we'll find out who it is."

"Could it be wolves or bears?" asked Beryl.

"Oh no," said Moonshine. "I don't think it's them."

Around the fallen tree there were lots of mushrooms and tasty roots. Beryl, Amber, and Dew nervously sniffed around for food, with Aunt Sissy standing guard very close to them while they foraged.

"H...how did you s...sense it?" Dew asked Beryl.

"*I* didn't feel or sense anything," puzzled Amber.

"I don't know. I didn't try, it just happened," Beryl replied.

"You're more wild pig than us," smiled Amber.

Beryl's nose was getting quite tough now, and she happily dug a root up and munched it down. She was reaching for another large, fresh-looking mushroom when, in a large shrubby bush straight in front of her, she saw something move. Was it a bird? It moved again. There, it twitched. It was an ear, twitching. The ear of an enormous creature—and it was watching her.

Beryl gasped and turned to Amber.

"It's a pig!" she cried.

Amber and Dew gasped. "Where?"

"There!" said Beryl, turning back and pointing with her snout, but it was gone. "It was huge! It was just there!" They all stared at the empty space where the pig had been moments before.

Aunt Sissy was at their side immediately. "What sort of pig?" she asked with an urgency that frightened them.

"I don't know," said Beryl, desperately trying to remember. "Hairy!"

"Quick! Back to the others!" Aunt Sissy said, looking around nervously.

"What's the matter?" asked Uncle Bert as they trotted up.

"Beryl's seen it! It was just here, only a few feet away from us!" said Aunt Sissy, her voice rising in panic. "Oh, Bert, what are we going to do? We're in the middle of nowhere! We're being tracked!"

"What did Beryl actually see?" Uncle Bert asked calmly.

"She saw a... lost pig!" Aunt Sissy wailed.

"Oh no!" said Uncle Bert, and all color drained away from his face.

THE LOST PIG

"What's a lost pig?" asked Amber.

"It's a terrible thing," said Uncle Bert. "They're pigs that are lost to the settlement. I saw one once, it couldn't even speak. I couldn't get near it. Luckily for me it was terrified," he said, shaking his head. "No pig can survive like that—we all need other pigs, none of us can live alone. They stay alive, but the loneliness drives them crazy."

"C…can't they get well again if they move back into a s…settlement?" asked Dew.

"I've never heard of any doing that. You see, they would have been banished. That's why they're out here," he said.

"They will probably have done something very bad to be thrown out," snorted Aunt Sissy.

"Could they be dangerous?" asked Beryl.

"They can be more dangerous than wolves or bears!" Aunt Sissy cried.

"Yes, I think we should be careful, but there's no need to panic," said Uncle Bert, frowning at Aunt Sissy.

"Will my mother be crazy?" Amber asked quietly.

Uncle Bert sighed. He'd been dreading this. "I'm afraid she probably is. She's been in the Vastness for a long time," he said gently. "I'm afraid there is very little hope for her. I don't mean she's necessarily gone bad or dangerous, although who knows? Lost pigs aren't like us. They lose their ability to communicate or even to recognize that other pigs are the same species. It's better that you forget her. You have Aunt Sissy and me, and we'll always be there for you. We love you very much," he said, and nuzzled her affectionately.

That night while Beryl, Amber, and Dew slept, Uncle Bert and Aunt Sissy kept watch.

By the morning it was beginning to rain.

"Did you see the lost pig last night?" asked Beryl.

"No, thank goodness," said Aunt Sissy. "Perhaps it got bored with us and wandered off."

"It'll be slower going today," said Uncle Bert, looking up at the rain. His trotters were covered in mud. "If it keeps up like this, it'll get very slippery. Maybe we should turn back."

"But we haven't found anywhere to settle yet," said Amber.

"We might not, even if we carry on," replied her aunt. She looked hopefully at Beryl. "What about you, wouldn't you rather go back?"

Beryl suddenly realized her trotters didn't hurt anymore and her legs didn't ache. "There might be the perfect spot just over the next mountain," she said, smiling. Aunt Sissy grunted.

"You're quite right, my dear," said Uncle Bert with a wink.

"The Chosen One has spoken!" boomed Moonshine. Aunt Sissy just tutted.

It was very slippery on the path up the mountainside, but eventually they managed to reach the peak.

"Well, I'll be…" said Uncle Bert, looking intently toward a dense part of the forest in the valley below. "That area's certainly worth a look! The trees are taller and it's in a hollow, with a stream for water, sheltered on three sides by cliffs. If we can get there, it has distinct possibilities. We'd be as snug and as safe as can be. And it has all this vast forest for foraging. This could be it, Sissy!"

"I hope so," sighed Aunt Sissy, distracted. "I don't think I can go on like this much longer."

"It's so beautiful," Amber breathed. "It looks perfect!"

"Do you think so?" said Aunt Sissy, looking for the first time. "Oh, I see what you mean. It does look good, doesn't it. Oh, Bert, could this be it?"

The Sisterhood were all chatting excitedly among themselves.

"The pathway down looks a bit tricky," muttered Uncle Bert.

"Come on!" called Aunt Sissy. "Let's see what it's like!" Already she was trotting down from the summit with a renewed spring in her step.

The pathway twisted down the side of a cliff. As they followed Aunt Sissy, slip-sliding down on the wet mud, the path narrowed and became more and more difficult. The ground was very slimy underfoot, and eventually the path was nothing but a ledge jutting out from the mountainside.

In places the edge of the path fell away abruptly.
Dislodged stones tumbled down, crashing into the
depths of the valley, and acting as a sober warning
of what might happen to them if they were
not careful.

Trotting along the ledge, Beryl felt the
hairs on her back rise. It wasn't because
of the perilous path, although that
did make her very nervous. Beryl
could feel it—she had no doubt
in her mind—she could sense
it as clear as spring water:
the lost pig was back.

"It's come back," said Beryl to the others.

Everyone stopped.

"Where?" said Amber, her eyes searching up the cliff, back the way they had come.

"I don't know, but it's watching," said Beryl.

"I don't like it, Bert!" Aunt Sissy shifted nervously, but Uncle Bert was sniffing the air.

"You can smell something?" Aunt Sissy sniffed the air urgently.

"Wolves! It's wolves!" cried Uncle Bert.

"Wolves?" gasped the Sisterhood.

"We can't run on this ledge! We're sitting ducks! They'll rip us apart!" wailed Aunt Sissy.

"Even if we could run, I don't know where they are, in front or behind us!" Uncle Bert sniffed the air frantically.

The pigs all froze. They stood in wide-eyed alarm on the narrow, slippery cliff path, not knowing which way to go.

VERY WILD THINGS

"We have to do something! Follow me," said Uncle Bert. "And try not to look down."

The words were hardly out of his mouth when a mass of rocks crashed and tumbled down, blocking the narrow ledge right in front of him.

"Blast!" shouted Uncle Bert.

Beryl looked up. Just for a second, she could have

sworn she saw something peeking out over the cliff top.

"Well, that's that!" said Uncle Bert. "We'll have to go back up and hope the wolves aren't behind us."

As they carefully turned and started back up the narrow twisting path, they heard a strange howling noise from beyond the pile of rocks.

"What's that?" said Beryl.

"W…WOLVES!" shouted Dew.

"RUN!" shouted Uncle Bert.

They ran as fast as they could on the precarious path, their pace quickening as the track widened.

"I think the fallen rocks must have stopped them!" panted Amber to Beryl.

"But not for long!" shouted Uncle Bert, and everyone galloped up to the top of the mountain and over the other side. Now Beryl was lagging behind, her lungs burning as she huffed and puffed for breath.

On the way down, running was more difficult. It was too slippery underfoot and Beryl tumbled and slid into the cover of the forest behind everyone else. The howling was getting louder again, and now there was excited yelping as the wolves picked up their scent.

"They're coming!" Aunt Sissy turned and shouted anxiously at Beryl.

Down and down the mountainside, through the trees, they scrambled and slid. Beryl could hardly run anymore. She couldn't catch her breath and the others were far in front of her. She saw Amber's tail disappear into the bushes way ahead.

The yelping became more and more frenzied.

Beryl could feel the wolves snarling and snapping right behind her. She dared not look around as she pushed her legs on and on, thudding out a gallop in the slippery mud. Despair tugged at her—she was alone and wheezing—but ahead was everything she had hoped for, and more. And it was her family, her dreams, and her freedom that took hold of her and drove her on through her pain. Sucking at the air for breath, she focused on the bushes in front, the bushes that had become her only goal, the bushes that had taken Amber and her family to safety.

The bushes came closer and closer until at last she was there. She heard a snort and teeth snap behind her and she felt a wolf's hot breath on her leg. With everything she had left, she dived into the bushes.

Tumbling down and down, head over tail she fell, finally splashing into a wide river. Bubbles and silence surrounded her as she somersaulted in the crystal water. As she broke the surface, the howling and yelping was now high above her.

All around her, the others were struggling for

air in the fast-flowing river.

"The river will take our scent and the wolves won't find us!" shouted Uncle Bert over the noise of the rushing water. They bobbed up and down with the flow of the river and the yelping changed to howling and became more distant, until it eventually faded away altogether.

The pigs paddled along, bouncing off rocks as they were swept away to safety. Slowly Beryl's wheezing subsided, and by the time she followed Uncle Bert and Aunt Sissy out of the river and onto the bank, she was breathing easily again. The pigs flopped down on the grassy bank and the Sisterhood collapsed as one mass in the shade of a giant willow.

Beryl lay on the ground, thankful she could at last relax. She'd never run so fast or for so long before, and it took some time for her lungs and legs to stop aching. She turned to the others.

"That lost pig pushed the rocks down the mountain. I saw it. I think it was trying to save us," she said.

"W…why would a lost pig save us?" asked Dew.

"I don't know," said Beryl.

There was a rustling in the bushes on the other side of the river. The pigs all sprang to their feet. A huge bear pushed through the undergrowth and stood facing them across the water.

Everyone stared in stunned silence.

Beryl had never seen such an enormous animal in her life.

"Don't move!" said Uncle Bert, his eyes as wide as two full moons. Before anyone could do or say anything, out of the bushes next to the bear appeared the lost pig.

It had a wild, crazy look in its eye. It stood there, next to the bear, as still as a rock, staring at them.

"Well, I'll be...," said Uncle Bert, not moving his moon-eyes a fraction.

"It's her!" cried Moonshine.

"Good heavens, so it is!" said Aunt Sissy.

"Who?" asked Beryl.

"My mother?" gasped Amber.

"Yes!" said Aunt Sissy.

THE LOST PIGS

The pigs stood facing the lost mother and the bear. No one moved a muscle or shifted their eyes from the pair for a moment.

"W...what do you think she w...wants?" whispered Dew.

"It's hard to tell," grunted Uncle Bert.

"She wants the Chosen One!" snorted Moonshine.

"She wants me," said Amber quietly.

"Then she can go on wanting!" hissed Aunt Sissy.

"Keep your eyes on the bear," instructed Uncle Bert, "but don't stare at it. Bears don't like that. Follow me and keep very close, and whatever you do, don't run."

They followed Uncle Bert stiffly and slowly, tight with tension. Close behind each other in a solid line, they crept along their side of the river and picked their way downstream. The bear and the lost mother watched them as they disappeared, but didn't move an inch.

Once they were out of sight, the pigs sploshed along the riverbank for what seemed like a lifetime.

"She's crazy, isn't she?" Amber said aloud to herself—she was working things out in her mind. Aunt Sissy looked at Amber with concern in her eyes.

"I'm afraid so," Aunt Sissy replied gently. "She isn't the same pig that she was. I'm so sorry."

"What if we tried to talk to her?" asked Beryl.

"She did save us from the wolves."

"You saw what she was like! Her eyes looked crazy!" cried Amber.

"And I can't see how we could talk to her with that bear there!" snorted Aunt Sissy. "You can't trust bears!"

"She doesn't *seem* dangerous. Maybe she's just curious about us," Beryl insisted, but Aunt Sissy and Amber gave her a look, and Beryl understood well enough to say no more on the subject.

They sploshed along in the shallow river all day. Beryl didn't see anywhere she recognized—none of the distant mountains looked even vaguely familiar. As the day passed, she began to realize that they were probably lost. The sun was low on the mountains when they eventually climbed out of the deepening

water and flopped onto the riverbank.

"We'll make camp here for the night. Why don't you, Dew, and Beryl find something to eat," said Uncle Bert to Amber. "Everything is always better on a full stomach."

"OK," said the little pig.

They could hear a faint roar in the distance.

"What's that?" asked Beryl.

"I know!" said Dew.

"Me, too!" said Amber. "Come on!"

They trotted along the path around the swelling river and down through a steep tunnel in the undergrowth. The roar was louder now, and as they crept along the tunnel it seemed to come from all around them. Amber and Dew charged ahead, down and out of the leafy tunnel.

"It's a waterfall!" squealed Amber in delight. Rainbows played in the waterfall's mist as the water fell into a large pool. Dew was first into the pool, followed closely by Amber. They splashed around, playing in the spray.

"Come on in, Beryl! It's lovely!" called Amber, but Beryl stood stock-still. For behind Amber and Dew the waterfall glistened, and there behind the waterfall stood the lost mother.

The lost mother stared at them through the cascading water, and she looked *really* crazy. Just as Beryl was starting to wonder how she had

followed them there, she was gone.

"Wait!" shouted Beryl. Jumping into the pool, she swam through the cascading water and out into the forest, after the lost mother.

"Beryl, no!" screamed Amber. Scrambling out of the water with Dew on her tail, she chased after Beryl through the waterfall and into the undergrowth on the other side.

THE LOST MOTHER

Amber and Dew sped after Beryl, and Beryl ran after the lost mother through the undergrowth. At last, the sow stopped and turned to face her pursuers, who stopped, too.

Beryl turned to her friend. "Talk to her, Amber!" she pleaded. "It may be your only chance!"

Amber stared into the crazy eyes of this large

lost pig. Was she dangerous?

"You're my mother!" Amber cried.

The lost mother stared at her.

"*Are* you my mother?" asked Amber.

"Sh…she is!" cried Dew.

"I think she wants to talk, but can't," said Beryl. Nervously, she stepped toward the lost mother.

The lost mother's eyes widened in panic. For a moment Beryl thought she would turn and run again. Beryl looked deeply into the eyes of the lost mother and saw terror staring back.

"Please stay," she said as gently as she could, and edged closer.

Slowly, Beryl sat down in front of the lost mother. She didn't really know what to do—it wasn't as if she had planned any of this. So, in the gentlest voice she could manage, she started to sing a song that she'd always known. Whenever she was frightened or panicky, this song had helped her. Perhaps it might help relax the lost mother now.

"Dark clouds cover the sun,
And the light has gone."

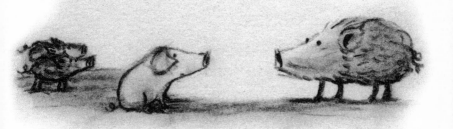

Amber came and sat beside Beryl and to Beryl's utter surprise, joined in her song.

"When the clouds part,
Letting light in my heart,
We'll wish for happiness.
You'll always be part of me,
We'll wish for happiness,
And one day we'll be free."

A tear rolled down the lost mother's face. The fear and madness in her eyes slowly melted away.

"You're not crazy," said Amber, frowning in puzzlement.

There was a crashing noise from behind them. Beryl, Amber, and Dew turned to see Uncle Bert puffing down the track.

"There you are!" he said. "You've had your aunt Sissy worried to the end of her bristles!"

When they turned back around, the lost mother had vanished.

FINDING OUT

As they all settled down for the night, the rain started.
Beryl couldn't get the picture of the lost mother out
of her head.

"Are you OK?" Amber asked.

"I don't know," said Beryl. "How did you know
my song?"

"I don't know," said Amber, screwing up her face

in thought. "I've always known it. Maybe it's just one of those songs that everyone knows."

"I…I've never heard it b…before," said Dew, "and my mom knows loads of songs, believe me!"

"My dad used to sing it to me, before he was taken," Beryl reminisced.

"W…where was he taken?" asked Dew.

"I think the farmers killed him," Beryl replied bitterly.

"Th…that's a…awful," said Dew, and they all fell silent. The rain poured down and they huddled up close under what little shelter they could find, and fell asleep.

It rained all night.

In the morning it was decided by Uncle Bert, Aunt Sissy, and the Sisterhood that they were indeed lost. Overnight, the river had swollen and turned into a torrent.

"We can't get back up that!" grunted Uncle Bert, staring at the whirlpools and eddies as the water swept past.

"But we must get back to the others!" insisted Moonshine. The Sisterhood chattered hysterically together.

"But we don't know where they are, and we can't use the river," Aunt Sissy said. "It's too deep and fast now."

"The stones will know!" Moonshine boomed.

"We must do the stone ritual."

All the Sisterhood murmured in approval.

A circle was formed, and the stone ritual performed, but it was hopeless. The ground was far too muddy.

"I've never seen it like this!" cried Moonshine. "Nothing! It indicates nothing. What are we to do?" The Sisterhood stood in silence staring at the stones, willing them to show the way.

"Enough of this!" grunted Uncle Bert. "We will just have to try and follow the path of the river back on higher ground."

"We shall get even more lost out there among the trees!" cried Moonshine.

"She's right, Bert," Aunt Sissy agreed. "Look up there. There's no way through. We'll never be able to follow the river now. We'll have to wait until it stops rising."

"At this time of year it could be weeks! The others will be long gone!" grunted Uncle Bert.

Everyone was quiet.

"The lost mother will know the way," thought Beryl, then looking up, she realized she'd said it aloud. Everyone was staring at her. She went pink.

"You're right!" said Amber, smiling.

"But she's crazy, my dears, we couldn't trust her," said Aunt Sissy gently. "And then there's the bear!"

"Been out here too long," Uncle Bert added.

"She's gone 'bear'!" Moonshine insisted, and the Sisterhood all repeated "Gone bear!" to settle the point, but ended up sounding like a flock of sheep.

"W…we have n…no ch…choice!" said Dew. "B…Beryl's right."

Everyone was silent again.

Then Moonshine and the Sisterhood huddled in a tight group, whispering.

Aunt Sissy and Uncle Bert began a mumbled conversation.

Amber, Dew, and Beryl just sat and thought. At last, Beryl broke the silence. "How can we get to talk to her?" she whispered.

"Maybe she would come to the waterfall again,"

Amber suggested.

"I…I don't think she'd come i…if everyone was th…there," said Dew, sneaking a peek at the others.

Just then Moonshine and the Sisterhood stood up. It seemed they had come to a decision.

"We feel," Moonshine began, "that the Chosen One should be the one to contact the lost mother."

Uncle Bert and Aunt Sissy stopped mumbling together and stared at Moonshine.

"Well, that's convenient, I must say!" Aunt Sissy snapped. "Doesn't matter that it's a wee bit dangerous then?" she snorted.

"I'm sure it won't be dangerous," Moonshine told her.

"Why don't *you* go and chat with her, then?" Aunt Sissy snorted.

"We, the Sisterhood," Moonshine smiled a reassuring smile, "feel this is why the Chosen One was chosen."

"Who was she chosen *by* exactly?" Aunt Sissy snapped.

"The stones," the Sisterhood crooned in unison.

"You can't send a piglet out there to talk to a crazy pig!" snorted Uncle Bert. "Have some decency!"

There was a long silence.

"I don't mind," said Beryl quietly. "I don't think the lost mother means us any harm. She's saved us once already. I think she wants to help us."

Everyone stared at her.

"I'll come with you," said Amber at last.

"M…me, too!" said Dew.

"I don't think that's necessary!" Moonshine said to Dew.

"I…it is!" insisted Dew firmly.

"Well, I don't like it!" Uncle Bert grunted.

"It may be the only way we can get back. We need her and she might be too frightened to help us if all the adults are around," said Amber.

"I hate to say it, Bert, but Amber's got a point," sighed Aunt Sissy. "It's the bear that worries me!"

BACK TO THE WATERFALL

Beryl, Amber, and Dew found their way back to the waterfall, while Uncle Bert and Aunt Sissy hid in the tunnel of undergrowth, just in case.

"I wonder if she'll come," said Amber.

They sat for ages, watching and waiting and trying not to fidget.

"She's here," whispered Beryl, and there behind

the cascading water was the lost mother, in the same spot she had been before.

"We need your help," Beryl called over the sound of the water.

"W…we're lost!" shouted Dew.

"Please help us!" begged Amber.

The lost mother walked around from behind the waterfall and stood on their side of the pool, right in front of them. There was no longer any sign of craziness in her eyes.

"You're my mother," said Amber, as if trying to convince herself.

Amber's mother spoke. "I didn't want to leave you; they made me. I thought it would be for the best." A tear trickled down her face.

"I know," said Amber.

"The bears said you'd come, that one day we would be together again," Amber's mother said.

"Will you help us?" asked Amber.

"Of course I will. That's what has kept me here all this time, waiting for this very moment. The bears predicted it. I don't know how, but I just hoped and dreamed they were right. I went really crazy with the loneliness, but I had to stay in case one day you came." A tear fell down her cheek, and Amber stepped up and nuzzled her gently.

"I've missed you so much," Amber's mom wept.

"Me, too!" cried Amber.

WHEN THINGS TURN OUT
AS THEY ARE

When they returned to the camp, Uncle Bert and
Aunt Sissy were already there, having crept back
ahead of them so as not to frighten Amber's mother.
The Sisterhood were a bit panic-stricken to see the
lost mother.

"It's OK," Amber reassured them.

"She's come to help us," said Beryl.

The Sisterhood said nothing.

It was Sissy who broke the silence.

"Hello, Ruby," she said.

"Hello, Sis," Amber's mom replied, and the Sisterhood relaxed with an audible sigh.

"Thank the hogs you're all right!" Uncle Bert exclaimed with a puff, as though he'd been holding his breath the whole time. The Sisterhood grunted in agreement, not really knowing who he meant—Amber, Beryl, and Dew or the lost mother—but it didn't seem to matter.

"S...so how do we g...get back to the E...Edge?" Dew asked Amber's mother.

"The bears will show us," said Amber's mom gently.

There was a loud gasp from the group.

"The bears!" Moonshine almost screamed. "That's your big plan! Oh no! No! NO! The crazy pig—OK! But no bears!"

As if summoned, a huge bear lumbered out of the thicket and stood behind Amber's mom. She smiled at it.

"If it hadn't been for the bears, I wouldn't be alive," she said. "You never can tell who your best friends will be."

Amber backed away from the bear nervously. Dew's, Aunt Sissy's, and Uncle Bert's bristles rose on their backs. Moonshine and the Sisterhood almost fell over each other as they moved away in panic.

"Beryl, come back!" cried Amber.

"It's OK," said Beryl, smiling at her. "I was frightened of *you* when we met, but you're not at all wild." She went up to the bear. "Thank you for agreeing to help us," she said.

"That's all right," grunted the bear.

WAY BACK

After what seemed to Beryl an awfully long time, the other pigs relaxed and even agreed that perhaps they weren't in imminent danger of being eaten.

Amber and Dew were the first, after Beryl, to smile shyly at the bear and get within pawing distance.

"A...are you really going to h...help us?" Dew asked.

"Yes," gruffed the bear, who was secretly starting to regret offering to help this bunch of ungrateful pigs.

Eventually, the pigs agreed to follow Amber's mother back to her den for the night and set off from there in the morning.

"Well, we really haven't a choice!" Moonshine hissed at one of the more frightened Sisterhood members.

It was a sentiment a lot of the pigs felt but hadn't voiced. They started the slow trek up the valley and away from the gushing river.

After some time, Amber's mother stopped at an arch in the bushes.

"Home," she said, and they followed her and the bear through the thicket and into the entrance of a cave, in which sat a couple of large bears.

All the pigs panicked, except for Amber's mom and Beryl. Everyone else froze to the spot, unable to move but desperate to dart back to the safety of the bushes. Bears were known to be aggressive, violent, wild beasts that pigs should be very frightened of. And here were two, sitting large as life in the cave's entrance!

Amber hid behind Beryl.

"It's OK, I'm sure they won't bite!" said Beryl.

"Will they be like that one?" asked Amber, looking at the large, kind bear with her mother.

"No, they'll be violently savage!" said Beryl.

"Really?" gasped Amber.

"No!" Beryl laughed.

The bear they had followed lurched forward into the cave, then looked over his shoulder at the pigs and grunted. Swinging up gracefully, he stood upright on his back legs and turned, coming out of

the darkness, splaying each of his huge front paws out toward them. His great claws looked sharp and menacing. He rolled back his lips to display a row of enormous, gleaming white teeth.

"We're not monsters, you know, we're just bears. GRRRR!" he roared, giving the Sisterhood the fright of their lives.

"Oh, Sam, I'm so sorry," said Amber's mom to the bear. "These pigs were brought up to be frightened of bears. There's no sense in it."

"No sense in it!" grunted Uncle Bert, keeping a watchful eye on Sam. "It's well known they attack us!" he hissed.

"When did you ever meet anyone attacked by a bear?" sighed Amber's mom, rolling her eyes skyward.

"Well…," grunted Uncle Bert, thinking hard.

The Sisterhood started whispering together.

"What about that spotty…"

"No, that was wolves!"

"Have you met anyone?"

"I can't think of anyone…"

"Come to think of it…I never have met anyone," said Aunt Sissy thoughtfully. "Or even heard of anyone meeting anyone who's been attacked, either…."

"That's because it's a myth," Amber's mother insisted firmly. "And these bears want to help you, not attack you."

"It goes too far against the grain!" grunted Uncle Bert. "Against everything we've been taught!"

The Sisterhood fell silent.

Beryl looked into Uncle Bert's eyes. "I was brought up to believe wild pigs would kill and eat me, but you haven't," said Beryl.

"Good gracious!" spluttered Uncle Bert. "What a dreadful thing to tell a piglet!" His eyes softened. "So you thought that," he said, pondering. "And you reckon it's the same with us and the bears, eh? Well, I suppose you've got a point, my dear. This chap seems friendly enough, that's for sure."

"Pigs!" gruffed Sam, dropping down on all fours, and he sauntered ahead into the cave, tut-tutting.

BEAR FACTS

"This could be perfect!" said Uncle Bert as he looked around the cave. "We could make a home here, Sissy."

"The others won't like it. What about Rule Number One?" whispered Aunt Sissy.

"Pah! I think we've had enough of rules, don't you?" He winked. "I'm sure the others will see sense." He strode up to Sam. "Would you mind calling a Council? I have something I want to discuss with your, er, clan," he said in an officious manner.

"Oh yeah?" sniggered Sam, scratching his ear. "Well, we bears don't do Councils. That's a pig thing."

"How do you come to decisions, then?" puffed Uncle Bert, not quite believing his ears.

"We don't bother," Sam sighed, rolling his eyes as he got up. "Pigs!" he gruffed as he strolled off, leaving Uncle Bert dumbfounded.

Uncle Bert sat down heavily next to Aunt Sissy.

"Really, that takes the cake! No organization, bears. I don't think it would work out here after all. We'll have to keep looking," he grunted.

"I think that might be best," Aunt Sissy agreed gently.

Everyone settled down for a restful sleep. The pigs slept in the cave entrance. Beryl sat looking out onto the valley below, and it struck her how

peaceful and harmonious it was. She saw Sam
sitting by a tree a little way from the cave. He was
looking at something in the lower branches. In the
half-dark it looked like a large bird. He appeared to
be talking to it.

Amber nuzzled her gently. It was time to sleep.

Morning arrived and the pigs were ready to start
back to the Edge.

Sam lolloped up to Amber's mom. It was the
signal everyone seemed to have been waiting for.

The other bears came out of the cave and, in

turn, came up to Amber's mom and gave her a soft farewell nuzzle. Beryl was struck by how gentle the huge bears were and realized that Amber's mom wouldn't be coming back—that this was obviously a final parting.

The herd of pigs followed Sam away from the cave and onto the path for the Edge. It was crisp and crunchy underfoot, a frosty morning that stood as a reminder of the cold winter that would be descending steadily over the forest in the weeks to come. Amber looked concerned, and Beryl asked her why.

"It takes a long time to dig out the dens for a settlement, and we'll have to start digging before the ground becomes too frozen in the big snow. If we don't find somewhere soon, it will be impossible," she explained.

"What happens if we don't find anywhere in time?" asked Beryl.

"You don't want to know—it would be bad! The big snow is really cold," said Amber.

Beryl plodded on and, throughout the day, hoped and prayed the other groups had had more luck in finding a suitable site for the new settlement.

The trek was slow going. There had been a lot of flooding in the last couple of days, and some of the paths had been swept away with the rush of water sweeping down parts of the mountain. By the time they made camp, Beryl saw that everyone was exhausted, except for Sam—he looked as if he could have bounded up to the top of the mountain and back without the slightest effort.

Beryl and Dew snuffled about eating roots and

mushrooms for their dinner. It was strange without Amber snuffling beside Beryl. Amber had been with her mom all day and Beryl missed her, but she didn't want to intrude on Amber getting to know her mom; it was something Beryl and Amber couldn't really do together. She liked Dew a lot, but it wasn't the same without her sister. That night, Dew and Beryl nested up into a tight huddle without uttering a word and fell fast asleep.

To Beryl, morning seemed to arrive as soon as she had fallen asleep. She lay on the grass next to Dew and felt she had been robbed of the night. She looked across the huddled pigs to her friend Amber, who was cuddled up with her mother. They looked so peaceful together, as though all those years apart had never happened.

Beryl felt a pang of jealousy—it stabbed at her suddenly and took her by surprise. It wasn't that she didn't like Amber's mother; quite the opposite, she thought she was wonderful. Nor that they were spending too much time together; after all, they had so much catching up to do. It was just that she felt she had lost something precious. Not her friendship with Amber—that was still very strong—but maybe an understanding of what it was like to be motherless in a world full of families. Beryl didn't want to feel jealous of Amber having a mom, but inside she wished she could have one, too.

Dew's eyes opened.

"O…oh no, i…it's morning al…already!" she moaned, and closed her eyes again.

All the pigs had the same difficulties getting up and preparing for another day of walking. There was a lot of grunting and snorting, but slowly the pigs got themselves together and set off for another grueling trek in the mud.

There was very little chattering as the day wore on, and everyone was close to collapse by the time the Edge came into view. As they descended the final mountain slope, it became obvious that there was only a tiny group of pigs standing at the Edge crossing. One of them was Colin.

"Where is everyone?" panted Aunt Sissy as she trotted up to him.

"They've all gone back," said Colin. "We waited for you. Then the river flooded, so we were stuck here. Some of the mothers were worried about the little ones with the big snow coming, and the others just lost heart. You took so long!" he explained.

"Didn't the other groups find anywhere?" Uncle Bert asked, looking at Colin and the little group and hoping his worst fears wouldn't be confirmed.

"I'm afraid not," said Colin. "Too many wolves."

"There were wolves where we were, too," said Aunt Sissy.

"I don't know what we shall do now. There aren't enough of us to start a settlement, and even if we did, it's getting too close to the big snow. I'm afraid it's absolutely hopeless!" Uncle Bert grunted.

"We can't go back across that either!" cried Aunt Sissy, and they all looked at the swollen river racing past them.

"Not all of us would be allowed back!" Uncle Bert grunted.

Just then Sam lumbered into Colin's view.

"BEARS!" he screamed, and the rest of the little Edge group panicked.

"It's OK, Colin, it's just Sam," said Amber calmly.

Sam strolled into the huddle of bristling pigs.

"We could try and live with the bears, I suppose, until the big snow melts," Uncle Bert grunted.

"Pah! Yeah, right!" Sam snorted.

"What does the Chosen One think we should do?" Moonshine turned to Beryl. The rest of the Sisterhood looked searchingly at Beryl, too.

"I don't know!" cried Beryl. "What do you think we should do, Sam?" she asked the bear.

"Why don't you just go to the other settlement?" said Sam. He really couldn't understand pigs; they just didn't make any sort of bear-sense at all. Amber's mom pushed through the crowd and looked at him.

"What other settlement, Sam? Why didn't you tell me about it before?" she asked.

"You never asked," said Sam, looking a bit puzzled. "The other other settlement."

"What other other settlement?" asked Uncle Bert.

"The one that isn't the settlement!" Sam groaned. He was getting bored with the way this conversation was going.

Everyone was snorting and grunting.

"Can you show us where it is?" asked Beryl above the noise.

Sam looked at Beryl with growing admiration. She had a bit more bear in her head than the others. Could this, at last, be a pig you could understand?

"You haven't been hanging out with these pigs long, have you?" he said.

"Er, no," said Beryl, a bit taken aback and a little embarrassed.

"Sure, we'll set off for the other settlement first thing tomorrow," he said, and then retreated to the tranquility of the trees.

Beryl felt very lonely that night. It might have been the exhaustion, or perhaps it was Amber spending so much time getting to know her mom, or that Dew was now snuggled up with hers. Beryl sat a little bit away from the others and watched the river flow past. There was no point in dwelling on not having a mother to love, it was just the way things were.

Sam came and sat beside her.

"I ain't got a mom either," he said softly.

"How do you know I haven't?" asked Beryl. She was quite taken with this gentle giant.

"We bears know everything, it's just the way it is," he said, chewing on a claw. "I guess that's why it's me hanging out with you pigs."

"Because you know everything?" asked Beryl, frowning, a little bit confused.

"No!" he groaned. "Not having a mom, it sort of sets you apart, you know?"

"Yeah," said Beryl. She had never heard it put so succinctly. "I feel I've been apart from everything my whole life," she sighed.

"There's good and there's bad to be had from it." He nodded, as if agreeing with himself.

"How do you mean?" Beryl asked. She couldn't see any good from not having a mother, even when she thought really hard about it.

"Well," said Sam, shifting his weight and lowering his voice. "Take your friend Dew's mother, Moonshine," he said, raising a paw as if Beryl might leap to her defense. "Nice enough pig, I'm sure, but would you want her as a mother?"

"N...no!" Beryl gasped, shocking herself at the speed of her response.

"Just the thought of it makes you stutter, eh?" Sam winked and his huge eyes twinkled. Beryl found herself smiling at his enormous kind face.

They curled up together, and Beryl buried her snout into his fluffy warm coat. They fell asleep together on the riverbank, set apart from the group and huddled on their motherless island.

BACK INTO THE VASTNESS

The morning was cold, and it wasn't much warmer by noon. Beryl was happy in the cold—she tended to get over-hot when she was walking. Amber trotted up and fell in beside her.

"Hi!" Amber cheerfully greeted her.

"Hi," replied Beryl, a bit distantly.

"I haven't seen much of you," Amber ventured.

"No, I've been a bit busy," said Beryl snootily, then instantly felt embarrassed. She should be happy for Amber.

"I'm sorry, but I've got a lot to talk about with Mom," Amber explained.

"I know, I'm sorry, too," said Beryl. "I just miss being with you, that's all."

"Why don't you come and talk to her, too?" tried Amber.

"She doesn't want to talk with me," said Beryl. "I'll be in the way."

"You won't be, you're my sister, after all!" said Amber. "I want you to like her."

"I do like her," Beryl replied as she plodded along. She desperately wanted to be happy for Amber, but Amber's mother had taken her place. She felt she would be intruding on some mother-daughter bonding if she tagged along. Things had changed forever and she was struggling to be happy about that. But maybe tagging along would help her get used to the way things were now—and she certainly did miss Amber a lot.

"OK, tonight I'll come and sleep with you both," she relented, just as Dew came up and joined them.

The three of them plodded up the mountain and down again. Aunt Sissy and Uncle Bert walked with them and chatted, lifting their spirits again and helping them with the relentless pace until the sun started to rest on the horizon.

Camp was made in a valley under an overhanging cliff, which was just as well because as soon as they got settled it started to rain. They all huddled together under the shelter of the overhang.

That night, as promised, Beryl stayed with Amber and her mom. An owl hooted hauntingly, and Sam came lumbering up and sat with them.

"What happened to my dad?" Amber was asking her mother.

"They made him leave. He didn't know that I was pregnant with you. I didn't tell him," she said.

"He was a pink," said Amber.

"Yes, he had escaped from a farm. The Council wouldn't let him stay," the sow remembered with a heavy heart. "I don't know what happened to him. I hoped so hard he'd be OK out here. I should have gone with him. I've sometimes regretted not going, but at the time I was too frightened and I was worried about you."

"Why didn't you try to find him when you were banished?" asked Amber.

"The bears told me that you would come. They foretold it, so I stayed and waited," she said, smiling. "And they were right."

Everyone sat quietly for a bit.

Then out of the blue Beryl had a horrible thought. "What if they won't let me in this other settlement?" Beryl said. "What if they have Rule Number One, as well?"

Amber stared at Beryl and realized she hadn't thought of the possibility of more rules.

"Won't be a problem," said Sam as he studied his claws lazily.

"Why?" Beryl asked as she looked at the bear's kind, fluffy face.

"They don't have that stupid rule," said Sam.

"How do you know?" asked Beryl.

"'Cause that's where that other pink pig you were just talking about went to. He lives there." Sam smiled reassuringly at Beryl.

"What?" gasped Amber's mom. "You knew all this time? Why didn't you tell me?"

"You never asked," groaned Sam. "Besides, you had to wait for Amber."

"How far is it to the other settlement? Will we make it before the big snow?" Beryl asked.

"Yeah, it's not too far now," said Sam. "But we gotta get past the Bad Lands first."

"The Bad Lands?" said Amber.

"Yeah, they're, er… bad," Sam grunted. He curled up next to Beryl, closed his huge eyes, rested an enormous paw on her, and fell fast asleep.

It rained all night long. It was still raining when everyone got ready to move in the morning.

Everybody, that is, except Sam. Sam was still fast asleep. The pigs crowded around him, wondering what to do.

"You wake him," Moonshine whispered to Beryl.

"Why me?" said Beryl.

Moonshine smiled a knowing smile. "You're the Chosen One," she crooned.

Beryl was just about to argue the point when the great bear stirred. "Go away!" he gruffed, turned over, and went back to sleep.

None of the pigs knew what to do, so they retreated, leaving the bear to sleep.

He slept through the whole day.

THE BAD LANDS

Some of the pigs were very mad, and whispered arguments and discussions punctuated the day.

But Beryl was glad to have the day off, especially since the rain didn't let up. She snoozed through the afternoon with Amber, Dew, and Amber's mom, Ruby.

The four of them rolled onto their backs and

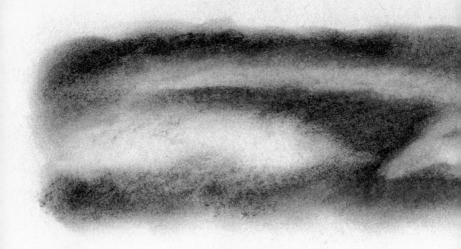

watched the rain clouds scud past.

"I remember a time when I'd sit or lie around all day. It seems so long ago now," Beryl pondered.

"D…do you miss it?" asked Dew.

Beryl laughed. "No! It was awful!"

They all watched the clouds above them changing shape.

"I can't wait to get settled into a den of our own, with both of you, and just do normal pig-things in our very own burrow," Ruby said, smiling dreamily at Amber and Beryl. Then suddenly something above them caught her eye. She gasped, "Look, it's a pig!"

Above them, a huge, pig-shaped cloud floated

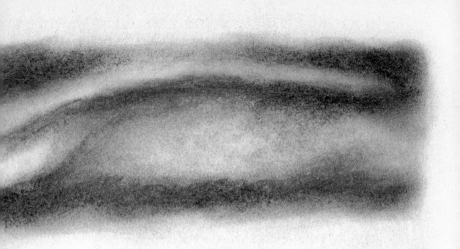

across the sky. They all watched as it stretched this way and that, transforming into a bear and then into a giant bird. But Beryl felt quite shaken. She wasn't really concentrating on the cloud. She stared at Ruby—had she heard her right?

"Can I really live with you?" Beryl squeaked, betrayed by the desperation in her voice.

"Where else, silly? You're my sister!" Amber frowned.

"We're your family, if you want us," smiled Ruby.

"Oh yes, I do!" gasped Beryl. It was the only thing she wanted; the very thought made her tremble. Then she frowned. "Only, I don't know what normal pig-things are."

"Nor do I, really, it's been so long since I've lived as a normal pig!" laughed Ruby.

Amber smiled. "I do!"

The setting sun bled red across the sky.

Sam gruffed.

"He's awake!" Beryl whispered.

Sam stretched and sauntered over to Beryl.

"Ready?" he said.

"Er, yeah," Beryl said, and she got to her feet, followed by Amber, Ruby, and Dew. When the other pigs saw them standing, they came over.

"It's a bit late now!" Uncle Bert said grumpily.

"What game do you think you're playing? We've been waiting all day!" Moonshine frowned at Sam.

The Sisterhood gathered around Moonshine looking very annoyed and grunting loudly. The relentless rain had frayed everyone's patience.

"Can't trust bears!" someone in the crowd grunted.

Sam stretched to his full height. "Are you ready, pigs?" he gruffed, scratching his belly.

"It's too dark to travel now, we can't see!" grumbled Uncle Bert.

"The darker the better," said Sam. "Coming or not?"

Moodily, everyone fell in behind Sam, Beryl, Amber, Dew, and Ruby as they set off on the path down the valley.

It was hard going in the fading light.

"Why are we traveling at night?" Beryl asked the kindly, lumbering bear.

"Can't cross the Bad Lands in daylight. Too dangerous," he said. In the distance, Beryl heard the sound of dogs barking.

"Why didn't you tell them that last night?" Beryl frowned.

"They didn't ask," gruffed Sam.

"Why is it that you don't tell anybody anything unless they ask?" Beryl was curious.

"If I did, I'd be here for the rest of my life! I told you, bears know everything," he huffed.

The trees thinned and the going became easier. A full moon rose in the night sky, dappling the

ground with an eerie blue light. Then, abruptly, the trees stopped. In front of them were the Bad Lands.

Farms and factories with lights glinting from their buildings followed the roads that crisscrossed the valley. Illuminated mechanical snakes chugged along tracks next to a river. The sound of barking dogs floated up from the valley. The air hummed with the distant rumble of cars and vans and the buzz of electricity pylons. Black and gray smoke belched from the factory chimneys, sweeping across the whole valley like a creeping cancer.

The Bad Lands stretched out as far as they could see. There seemed no end to the ugliness of it.

An owl swooped in the air above them.

"We're going to cross *that*?" Uncle Bert gulped. He tried to keep the disbelief out of his voice.

"Yup," said Sam.

"Can't we go around it?" Uncle Bert pleaded.

"There is no 'around it'—this is the narrowest part of the Bad Lands," said Sam. "Darkness is our friend."

As if it had heard the giant bear, the moon kindly slipped behind a cloud. Hiding in the shadows of the hedgerows, they moved quietly together in a tight line. No one spoke, and it wasn't until they had safely crept past the first barn that Beryl remembered to breathe.

She could smell the familiar smell of pink pigs and manure. She looked up at the hangarlike barn and realized it was probably full of factory pigs, pigs just like her, but with no future.

"Come on!" hissed Sam, and she followed him along the hedge until they came to an opening. Stretching out in front of them was a broad, smooth strip of blackness. Headlights flashed past in both directions, issuing a roar and a puff of wind as they raced along. Then there was nothing but stillness and the dark.

"Quick!" hissed Sam, and he dashed across the road and disappeared into the hedge on the other side. Beryl was right behind him, followed hotfoot by the rest of the pigs.

Once on the other side, they clambered down into a ditch and followed it along the edge of a meadow. From above their heads, on the other side of the hedge, came the roaring and whoosh of the traffic. They sloshed along the ditch as it led them away from the road and left the noise of traffic behind.

It wasn't long before they reached another road, and then another. Sneaking past barns, yards, and farmhouses, they managed to keep away from barking and snarling dogs. The whole time, an owl swooped and glided above them. They crossed cabbage and lettuce fields, and meadows with cows and sheep in them. As they were skirting one muddy field they saw a lot of pigs who lived in little bunkers. Some of the factory pigs were very close, just on the other side of the fence.

"They look a bit like you," Amber whispered to Beryl as they crept past.

"SHHH!" hissed Sam, but it was too late. The factory pigs heard them. There was a snort and a cry as the pink pigs saw the long line of wild pigs.

"Help! Wild pigs!" one screamed. They started to stampede to the other side of the muddy field, toward a cluster of buildings, snorting and wailing. The pink pigs yelled and screamed as though their very lives depended on it. "Help! Help!" The noise they created could be heard over the whole valley. Dogs started barking in one of the buildings and a human shout rang out.

"Come on!" shouted Sam. His voice broke the stunned silence of the others. They ran behind him as fast as they could along the fence and down into a ditch, splashing through the sludge. On and on they ran. The concentration of buildings and concrete became denser, and as they left the barking dogs behind they slowed to a trot. They crept between yards, factories, truck parking lots, sheds, and outbuildings, keeping as much as they could to anything natural, like undergrowth or hedges.

Silently, terrified, they swam to the other side of a river that stank of metal and oil and had garbage strewn along its banks. On the far side they waited, hiding in the garbage, watching the steel tracks and waiting for the illuminated mechanical snakes to chug out of sight.

At last they managed to cross into a strange little meadow where lots of rectangular stones stood among grass and shrubbery. An owl swept into a tree in the middle of the strange meadow. The roar of traffic noise grew with every step, until it seemed it couldn't get any louder.

Sam stopped at a gap in a wall made up of loose stones. Beryl moved beside him and peeked out at a huge, brightly lit road with columns of vehicles speeding both ways along it. Hundreds of cars and trucks continuously rushed past. This road was bigger than any of the roads they had crossed so far.

"How ever are we going to cross that?" Beryl whispered despairingly.

"We'll have to wait," said Sam.

And they did, huddled in among the shadows of the rectangular stones and shrubs, in this tranquil island in the middle of the roar and buzz and fumes of human destruction.

While they waited, the pigs rolled in the grass,

trying to rub off the greasy oil that had stuck to their skins when they'd crossed the river.

"Shhh!" hissed Sam. "There'll be time for that later!"

The pigs muttered, but they stopped rolling around all the same.

As the night wore on, one by one the lights in the buildings went out. Dogs stopped barking and the roar of the traffic died down until it was almost quiet. Only the buzz of the pylons and the chugging of the snakes and the occasional hooting of an owl punctured the silent night.

There hadn't been any headlights for some time when Sam pulled himself to his feet and peeked out through the gap in the wall. The pigs crowded around him, eager to be off. Everybody was ready; no one liked being stuck in the Bad Lands.

With a powerful leap, Sam sprang into the road, followed closely by Beryl and the others. They charged across the black expanse, leaped over the median and onto the second black strip, galloping for the safety of the far hedge.

Beryl heard a whooshing sound. Suddenly headlights were upon them. Beryl couldn't see anything but dazzling white light. She froze.

"Don't look at them!" shouted Sam, and he leapt into the hedge. Beryl shut her eyes and ran as fast as her legs would go. An almighty screeching noise screamed through the air, followed by a sickening thud. Beryl opened her eyes. She was through the hedge. Sam was next to her, looking over her and through the gap they'd just made. His face was frozen in a scream. Beryl followed his eyes. There, in the middle of the black expanse, lay Ruby, Amber's mother, sprawled out on the road. The car was turned sideways, farther down the road, headlights beaming into the hedge. Amber lunged toward her stricken mother with a wail of despair.

"She's dead," Aunt Sissy said in a hollow, shocked voice. "Come on, my dear, there is nothing we can do here." She nuzzled Amber, but Amber didn't seem to hear. She stood over her mother's body and wept.

"We have to go," Uncle Bert insisted gently.

Beryl heard another whooshing noise.

"Run!" she screamed, just as the headlights lit up the group. Amber froze in the beam of the lights.

The screech of tires rang through the air. Pigs stampeded past as the screeching grew louder. Beryl stared at the still figure caught in the lights.

"RUN! Please, Amber, RUN!" she screamed until her throat closed up. But Amber stood, frozen. Beryl lurched forward into the gap, but car lights dazzled her as they spun past with a deafening squeal and the acrid smell of burning.

Then there was darkness. Beryl couldn't see as she desperately peered through the hedge. As her sight returned she saw Amber, still as stone in the middle of the black expanse.

"AMBER!" she yelled, and this time Amber responded. She turned and ran as fast as she could behind Beryl, Sam, and the stampeding pigs. Away from the screeching, away from the whooshing, away from the headlights, away from destruction and the car that had left her mother dead in the middle of the road. They ran and ran, stumbling with panic and grief in the dark. Out in the open, across meadows and roads, they ran and ran, until they couldn't run anymore. Finally, they stumbled into the cover of the trees and out of the Bad Lands, flopping onto the ground among the comforting shadows.

Only then did Amber cry. She cried for what could have been, for the wrong that had been done, for the loss she felt. She wailed into the night with the grief of a daughter who has lost everything, who has had everything taken from her. She cried because she couldn't understand why any of it should be. She was angry and sad—and she was motherless again.

Uncle Bert and Aunt Sissy looked worn beyond their years. They tried to comfort Amber.

"She pushed me out of the way!" Amber cried, and the guilt of it consumed her.

Beryl nuzzled up to her. There was nothing she could think of to say to help her friend in her grief, so she stayed silent.

Sam came up and nuzzled Amber, too.

"She loved you beyond anything else," he said quietly.

"I got her killed!" wailed Amber through her tears.

"No," he said, sternly. "She saved you. I saw it happen. You would have *both* been killed." He cuddled her while she sobbed.

Aunt Sissy and Uncle Bert enveloped her and Beryl in a protective huddle, a pig huddle, that could soothe and protect the vulnerable in their time of greatest need.

After everyone had rested for a bit, Sam stood. The faintest hint of dawn softened the moon shadows. It was time to push on. Beryl gently nudged Amber, and Amber stood beside her but was miserably distant.

Beryl was relieved to be leaving the Bad Lands behind, with all their destruction, noise, and smell. It helped her fight the exhaustion, to know every step forward was one more step away from that hell.

It was a long, hard day for all of them. The youngest piglets started to look as if they wouldn't make it. Sam, members of the Sisterhood, Uncle Bert, and Aunt Sissy took turns in carrying them for part of the way. Everyone except Sam was plodding now; no one had the energy to even talk.

"I can't go on!" cried Amber, and she collapsed in a heap on the path. No one could go on—apart from Sam, everyone was beat.

BEN

Beryl flopped down heavily next to her sister. She ached all over. Amber sobbed into Beryl's shoulder and Beryl wondered if she would ever see her friend happy again.

An icy chill whipped through the woods.

"Enough is enough!" Moonshine grumbled.

"Perhaps we should camp here, and go on in the

morning," offered Aunt Sissy.

"Go on where? That bear's got us lost! I don't know why we trusted him!" Moonshine boomed.

The Sisterhood grunted and snorted, glaring angrily at Sam.

"My babies won't make it without shelter. We can't camp here!" cried a sow.

A snowflake fluttered down and melted on Beryl's nose.

"Heavens above! It's snowing!" grunted Uncle Bert. He looked old and worn.

"We're all lost!" wailed Moonshine dramatically.

"LOST!" wailed the Sisterhood.

"You're frightening my babies!" snapped the sow, desperately trying to shelter the shivering piglets.

Sam lumbered up to the sow and sat down next to her. With his great paws he gathered the piglets into the warmth of his furry stomach.

"He's going to eat them!" screamed Moonshine. "Leave those poor piglets alone, you beast!" And she lurched toward Sam.

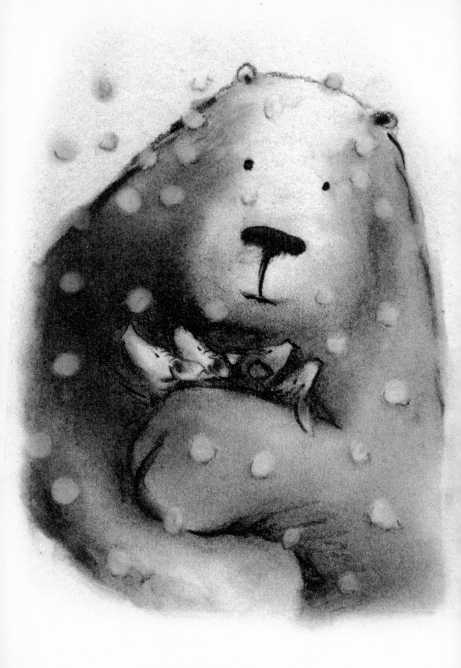

"Leave them alone!" The Sisterhood joined in with the attack, frowning and stamping on the ground in front of him.

Sam didn't seem to notice them. An owl swooped high above the trees, and Sam watched it glide as he cuddled the frozen piglets.

Moonshine and the angry Sisterhood surrounded him, snorting and grunting aggressively.

"He's protecting them," Beryl tried to explain, and she pushed with her last strength through the mob to face Moonshine. But Moonshine's eyes were sparkling with excitement and her mouth was frothing with anger.

"It's a bear trick! He got us lost so he can eat us all, one by one!" she yelled at the mob.

The Sisterhood grunted and snorted in agreement.

"STOP, MOM!" screamed Dew. "JUST STOP!"

Moonshine stopped, shocked. Stunned, she met Dew's angry stare.

The Sisterhood stopped.

Sam was still watching the owl and rocking the piglets.

Amber was sobbing and Uncle Bert looked haggard and old.

Colin and the Edge group looked desperate.

Is this the end? thought Beryl. But she stopped short of asking the bear, as she realized how frightened she was by the thought of what the answer might be.

She looked at the path they had come along. Snow fell in thick swirls around them. She looked at the way they were heading, up a narrow path.

Beryl could just make out a clearing through the swirls of snow. And there, in the clearing on the hilltop above them, was a shadow, the shifting shadow of something on the path.

Out of the white blizzard a huge, muscular pink pig came toward them.

"You're here at last!" he boomed as he ran, gathering speed as he came down the hill. It looked as if he had no way of stopping in time. Just as Beryl braced herself for the collision, he skidded to an abrupt halt.

"I thought you'd never get here!" he exclaimed, his eyes twinkling at the group, searching the faces of each of the pigs. He spotted Uncle Bert.

"Bert!" he exclaimed, and beamed a magical smile, which gave way immediately to a look of concern. "Is Ruby with you?" he asked, craning over Bert to search the pigs farther back.

"I'm afraid not, Ben," said Uncle Bert, looking back with sadness. "She didn't make it."

Ben the pink pig stood motionless, suddenly rooted to the spot, all laughter and sparkle draining from his eyes.

"It was a terrible thing," muttered Uncle Bert. Then, looking intensely at Ben, he said, "We need to talk, but we're all exhausted now."

Ben straightened and tried to shudder off the tragic news of Ruby. He looked across at the crushed figure of Uncle Bert.

"Of course. Follow me, you must all be done in. It's not far now," he said, and he led the tired, stumbling pigs through the clearing, along a twisting path and into the other settlement.

THE OTHER SETTLEMENT

Although the other settlement was dug out of the earth just like the old settlement, it had a very different feel to it. Beryl noticed at once that not only were the pigs a mixture of all kinds of pig, but that there were other animals, too—goats, rabbits, deer and even pheasants. There was a lively, slightly chaotic scene of animals coming and going about their sometimes noisy business.

"How did he know we were coming?" Beryl asked Sam.

"The owls told him. I asked them for help," said Sam quietly.

The pigs were very welcoming and showed everyone where they could curl up and sleep. Ben led Sam, Beryl, Amber, Uncle Bert, and Aunt Sissy into his den.

"Make yourselves at home," he said, and retreated out of the doorway they had just come through. Beryl was so tired, she could hardly make her way across the burrow to flop down with Amber.

"Do you think he's my dad?" Amber yawned, looking at Beryl.

"Ben?" Beryl asked, surprised. She noticed how awful her friend looked.

"He is," Aunt Sissy said gently. "But he doesn't know yet. Let's all get some sleep and things will be sorted out tomorrow."

"It's amazing what a bit of sleep can do," Sam

added softly. "Sleep and time." And that was the last thing Beryl heard until she woke, blinking the sleep from her eyes.

Ben was standing over her, and daylight streamed into the cozy den. He was studying her.

Beryl looked at him, puzzled. He continued to look at her. Beryl was about to ask him what he was staring at, when for the first time she saw something familiar in his face. Looking at the hairy, solid features, it was definitely there. It was his eyes she recognized. There

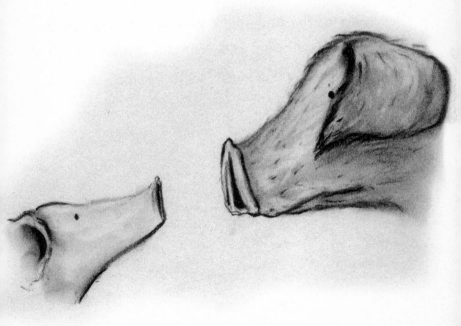

was nothing recognizable about this large, stocky, and hairy pig other than his eyes. And like pulling a root out of the mud, his features gradually became more familiar. Bit by bit, the face from her past came slowly into focus. Changed by time and buried under muscle and hair, it was still there in this face.

Beryl gasped.

Ben gasped, too.

"B…Beryl?" he stammered, disbelieving his own eyes.

"Dad?" Beryl croaked.

Their surprise and shock gave way to enormous smiles of recognition and reunion as they fondly nuzzled each other.

A NEW BEGINNING

Beryl's and her father's excited nuzzling woke up the others.

"This is Amber, my sister." Beryl beamed. "I think she's your daughter, too."

Ben swung around and took in this small pig with his intense gaze.

"Ruby," he thought aloud, and gasped.

"She was my mom," Amber said, and felt a lump in her throat and tears welling in her eyes.

"You poor piglet," he said, and nuzzled her gently. "Ruby was pregnant! Of course! That's why she wouldn't come!" he said, solving an ancient puzzle that had obviously troubled him greatly. He stood back and looked at them both. "Two daughters!" he exclaimed. With a huge and charming smile, his eyes twinkling with excitement, he said, "I'm so lucky!"

Suddenly, all made sense to Beryl.

"We really *are* sisters!" she laughed. For the first time since the tragedy, Amber smiled.

They joined Sam, Uncle Bert, Aunt Sissy, Dew, Moonshine, and all the pigs that had gathered outside. For the first time in her life, Beryl felt that she truly belonged. She didn't stand out in any way; there were pigs of all different types and sizes.

"There don't seem to be any rules here," she whispered to Sam.

"No, only respect for one another," he smiled. "The forest is changing and animals that cut themselves off from one another, like in the old settlement, will die."

"Why?" asked Beryl, shocked.

"Humans. They are destroying everything, cutting down the trees, turning everywhere into the Bad Lands. That old settlement will be wiped out in a couple of years when they chop the forest down. The pigs there would know about it if they hadn't cut themselves off from the rest of us. They could learn a thing or two from you," he said, and he shook his great head.

"Why me?" asked Beryl, puzzled.

"Because you don't let fear stop you from trying new things," Sam said, smiling. "Back in that truck you had a choice, and the choice you made was for freedom. Even though you were frightened of the unknown, it didn't stop you. The pigs in the old settlement, like Gruff and the others, allow fear to rule their lives, and it will kill them."

Beryl gaped at the kind, fluffy face. "How did you know about the truck, and Gruff...?"

Sam chuckled.

"You really do know everything!" gasped Beryl.

"Yeah! And here's a tip from someone who knows everything—we all need each other, that's for sure!" And the bear beamed an enormous smile.

An owl flapped down into a tree on the edge of the gathering.

Moonshine and the Sisterhood came and stood close to Beryl.

"I knew you were the Chosen One!" Moonshine said in her ear. "It's been proven! You saved us all!" she boomed, so everyone turned and looked.

"Saved us all!" bleated the Sisterhood.

Beryl went quite pink.

"I wasn't chosen; I didn't save anyone," Beryl said firmly. "Sam saved us. You were horrid to him, but he still did it."

Moonshine and the Sisterhood looked at the kind bear, and suddenly, for the first time that Dew could remember, her mother looked embarrassed.

"I...I'm so sorry, y...you've done so much for us," Moonshine stuttered to Sam. The Sisterhood looked

at the ground, grunting approval while shuffling their trotters.

"It's OK," said Sam, and he looked at Beryl with enormous fondness. "I must go back in a day or two," he said quietly to her, "but I'll come again soon."

Beryl could feel a tear forming in her eye. "I'll miss you," she croaked.

"Pigs!" he gruffed gently.

Beryl sat with Amber and looked into her sister and best friend's face, and hoped that in time she would be happy again. Amber had found and then lost her mother, and although the rest of her family—Beryl, her dad, Uncle Bert, and Aunt Sissy—loved her dearly, Beryl wondered if it would be enough. Sleep and time was what Sam had said, and those words echoed through her head.

Then Amber smiled at her.

Beryl smiled back, full of a very special feeling, the feeling of being a sister and a daughter, the feeling of being part of a family. When she looked into her sister's eyes, she was overcome by a powerful burst of love that bounced between them—her dad, Uncle Bert and Aunt Sissy, Moonshine, Dew, the Sisterhood, and Sam the bear. She had finally found her home. Home with family, home with her greatest friends, a home that made everything possible.

A home with a future.